BASIL THOMSON
A MURDER IS ARRANGED

SIR BASIL HOME THOMSON (1861-1939) was educated at Eton and New College Oxford. After spending a year farming in Iowa, he married in 1889 and worked for the Foreign Service. This included a stint working alongside the Prime Minister of Tonga (according to some accounts, he *was* the Prime Minister of Tonga) in the 1890s followed by a return to the Civil Service and a period as Governor of Dartmoor Prison. He was Assistant Commissioner to the Metropolitan Police from 1913 to 1919, after which he moved into Intelligence. He was knighted in 1919 and received other honours from Europe and Japan, but his public career came to an end when he was arrested for committing an act of indecency in Hyde Park in 1925 – an incident much debated and disputed.

His eight crime novels featuring series character Inspector Richardson were written in the 1930's and received great praise from Dorothy L. Sayers among others. He also wrote biographical and criminological works.

Also by Basil Thomson

BASIL THOMSON

A MURDER IS
ARRANGED

With an introduction by
Martin Edwards

DEAN STREET PRESS

Published by Dean Street Press 2016

All Rights Reserved

First published in 1937 by Eldon Press as
A Murder Arranged

Cover by DSP

Introduction © Martin Edwards 2016

ISBN 978 1 911095 81 1

www.deanstreetpress.co.uk

Introduction

SIR BASIL THOMSON's stranger-than-fiction life was packed so full of incident that one can understand why his work as a crime novelist has been rather overlooked. This was a man whose CV included spells as a colonial administrator, prison governor, intelligence officer, and Assistant Commissioner at Scotland Yard. Among much else, he worked alongside the Prime Minister of Tonga (according to some accounts, he *was* the Prime Minister of Tonga), interrogated Mata Hari and Roger Casement (although not at the same time), and was sensationally convicted of an offence of indecency committed in Hyde Park. More than three-quarters of a century after his death, he deserves to be recognised for the contribution he made to developing the police procedural, a form of detective fiction that has enjoyed lasting popularity.

Basil Home Thomson was born in 1861 – the following year his father became Archbishop of York – and was educated at Eton before going up to New College. He left Oxford after a couple of terms, apparently as a result of suffering depression, and joined the Colonial Service. Assigned to Fiji, he became a stipendiary magistrate before moving to Tonga. Returning to England in 1893, he published *South Sea Yarns*, which is among the 22 books written by him which are listed in Allen J. Hubin's comprehensive bibliography of crime fiction (although in some cases, the criminous content was limited).

Thomson was called to the Bar, but opted to become deputy governor of Liverpool Prison; he later served as governor of such prisons as Dartmoor and Wormwood Scrubs, and acted as secretary to the Prison Commission. In 1913, he became head of C.I.D., which acted as the enforcement arm of British military intelligence after war broke out. When the Dutch exotic dancer and alleged spy Mata Hari arrived in England in 1916, she was arrested and interviewed at length by Thomson at Scotland Yard; she was released, only to be shot the following year by a French firing squad. He gave an account of the interrogation in *Queer People* (1922).

Thomson was knighted, and given the additional responsibility of acting as Director of Intelligence at the Home Office, but in 1921, he was controversially ousted, prompting a heated debate in Parliament: according to *The Times*, "for a few minutes there was pandemonium". The government argued that Thomson was at odds with the Commissioner of the Metropolitan Police, Sir William Horwood (whose own career ended with an ignominious departure fromoffice seven years later), but it seems likely be that covert political machinations lay behind his removal. With many aspects of Thomson's complex life, it is hard to disentangle fiction from fact.

Undaunted, Thomson resumed his writing career, and in 1925, he published *Mr Pepper Investigates*, a collection of humorous short mysteries, the most renowned of which is "The Vanishing of Mrs Fraser". In the same year, he was arrested in Hyde Park for "committing an act in violation of public decency" with a young woman who gave her name as Thelma de Lava. Thomson protested his innocence, but in vain: his trial took place amid a blaze of publicity, and he was fined five pounds. Despite the fact that Thelma de Lava had pleaded guilty (her fine was reportedly paid by a photographer), Thomson launched an appeal, claiming that he was the victim of a conspiracy, but the court would have none of it. Was he framed, or the victim of entrapment? If so, was the reason connected with his past work in intelligence or crime solving? The answers remain uncertain, but Thomson's equivocal responses to the police after being apprehended damaged his credibility.

Public humiliation of this kind would have broken a less formidable man, but Thomson, by now in his mid-sixties, proved astonishingly resilient. A couple of years after his trial, he was appointed to reorganise the Siamese police force, and he continued to produce novels. These included *The Kidnapper* (1933), which Dorothy L. Sayers described in a review for the *Sunday Times* as "not so much a detective story as a sprightly fantasia upon a detective theme." She approved the fact that Thomson wrote "good English very amusingly", and noted that "some of his characters have real charm." Mr Pepper returned in *The Kidnapper*, but in the same year, Thomson introduced his most important character, a Scottish policeman called Richardson.

Thomson took advantage of his inside knowledge to portray a young detective climbing through the ranks at Scotland Yard. And Richardson's rise is amazingly rapid: thanks to the fastest fast-tracking imaginable, he starts out as a police constable, and has become Chief Constable by the time of his seventh appearance – in a book published only four years after the first. We learn little about Richardson's background beyond the fact that he comes of Scottish farming stock, but he is likeable as well as highly efficient, and his sixth case introduces him to his future wife. His inquiries take him – and other colleagues – not only to different parts of England but also across the Channel on more than one occasion: in *The Case of the Dead Diplomat*, all the action takes place in France. There is a zest about the stories, especially when compared with some of the crime novels being produced at around the same time, which is striking, especially given that all of them were written by a man in his seventies.

From the start of the series, Thomson takes care to show the team work necessitated by a criminal investigation. Richardson is a key connecting figure, but the importance of his colleagues' efforts is never minimised in order to highlight his brilliance. In *The Case of the Dead Diplomat*, for instance, it is the trusty

Sergeant Cooper who makes good use of his linguistic skills and flair for impersonation to trap the villains of the piece. Inspector Vincent takes centre stage in *The Milliner's Hat Mystery*, with Richardson confined to the background. He is more prominent in *A Murder is Arranged*, but it is Inspector Dallas who does most of the leg-work.

Such a focus on police team-working is very familiar to present day crime fiction fans, but it was something fresh in the Thirties. Yet Thomson was not the first man with personal experience of police life to write crime fiction: Frank Froest, a legendary detective, made a considerable splash with his first novel, *The Grell Mystery*, published in 1913. Froest, though, was a career cop, schooled in "the university of life" without the benefit of higher education, who sought literary input from a journalist, George Dilnot, whereas Basil Thomson was a fluent and experienced writer whose light, brisk style is ideally suited to detective fiction, with its emphasis on entertainment. Like so many other detective novelists, his interest in "true crime" is occasionally apparent in his fiction, but although *Who Killed Stella Pomeroy?* opens with a murder scenario faintly reminiscent of the legendary Wallace case of 1930, the storyline soon veers off in a quite different direction.

Even before Richardson arrived on the scene, two accomplished detective novelists had created successful police series. Freeman Wills Crofts devised elaborate crimes (often involving ingenious alibis) for Inspector French to solve, and his books highlight the patience and meticulous work of the skilled police investigator. Henry Wade wrote increasingly ambitious novels, often featuring the Oxford-educated Inspector Poole, and exploring the tensions between police colleagues as well as their shared values. Thomson's mysteries are less convoluted than Crofts', and less sophisticated than Wade's, but they make pleasant reading. This is, at least in part, thanks to little touches of detail that are unquestionably authentic – such as senior officers' dread of newspaper criticism, as in *The Dartmoor Enigma*. No other crime writer, after all, has ever had such wide-ranging personal experience of prison management, intelligence work, the hierarchies of Scotland Yard, let alone a desperate personal fight, under the unforgiving glare of the media spotlight, to prove his innocence of a criminal charge sure to stain, if not destroy, his reputation.

Ingenuity was the hallmark of many of the finest detective novels written during "the Golden Age of murder" between the wars, and intricacy of plotting – at least judged by the standards of Agatha Christie, Anthony Berkeley, and John Dickson Carr – was not Thomson's true speciality. That said, *The Milliner's Hat Mystery* is remarkable for having inspired Ian Fleming, while he was working in intelligence during the Second World War, after Thomson's death. In a memo to Rear Admiral John Godfrey, Fleming said: "The following suggestion is used in a book by Basil Thomson: a corpse dressed as an airman, with despatches in his pockets, could be dropped on the coast, supposedly from a parachute that has failed. I understand there is no difficulty in obtaining corpses at the Naval Hospital, but, of course, it would have to be a fresh one." This clever idea became the basis for "Operation Mincemeat", a plan to conceal the invasion of Italy from North Africa.

A further intriguing connection between Thomson and Fleming is that Thomson inscribed copies of at least two of the Richardson books to Kathleen Pettigrew, who was personal assistant to the Director of MI6, Stewart Menzies. She is widely regarded as the woman on whom Fleming based Miss Moneypenny, secretary to James Bond's boss M – the Moneypenny character was originally called "Petty" Petteval. Possibly it was through her that Fleming came across Thomson's book.

Thomson's writing was of sufficiently high calibre to prompt Dorothy L. Sayers to heap praise on Richardson's performance in his third case: "he puts in some of that excellent, sober, straightforward detective work which he so well knows how to do and follows the clue of a post-mark to the heart of a very plausible and proper mystery. I find him a most agreeable companion." The acerbic American critics Jacques Barzun and Wendell Hertig Taylor also had a soft spot for Richardson, saying in *A Catalogue of Crime* that his investigations amount to "early police routine minus the contrived bickering, stomach ulcers, and pub-crawling with which later writers have masked poverty of invention and the dullness of repetitive questioning".

Books in the Richardson series have been out of print and hard to find for decades, and their reappearance at affordable prices is as welcome as it is overdue. Now that Dean Street Press have republished all eight recorded entries in the Richardson case-book, twenty-first century readers are likely to find his company just as agreeable as Sayers did.

Martin Edwards

www.martinedwardsbooks.com

Chapter One

It was the duty of Chief Constable Richardson's clerk to run through the morning papers and call his chief's attention to any case in which the help of New Scotland Yard (C.I.D. Central) might be invoked. The clerk, a patrol named Walter Goodwin, brought in a number of newspaper cuttings one morning in December.

"Anything special?" asked Richardson.

"Not in the metropolitan area, sir, but there's a case at Marplesdon in Surrey that I think you ought to read." Richardson took up the cutting from a popular paper and read:

"MYSTERIOUS SHOOTING CASE NEAR MARPLESDON, SURREY.

"In the early hours of yesterday morning the body of a young woman in evening dress was found lying in Crooked Lane, which traverses Marplesdon Common. She has been identified as Miss Margaret Gask, one of the guests at Scudamore Hall where Mr Forge is entertaining a house party for Christmas. She had been shot through the head. None of the other guests was able to explain why she should have been in Crooked Lane during the night. Apparently she had said good night and retired to her room just before midnight. Her bed had not been slept in."

"This is just the sort of case in which the chief constable of Surrey may ask for help from Central," said Richardson. "Who have we got available?"

His clerk reflected. "I believe that Detective Inspector Dallas has about cleared up that case in Chelsea. His report is coming in to you, sir."

"Very well; we must sit tight until we have an application from the Surrey chief constable."

"Very good, sir."

"You might tell Mr Dallas that probably he will be wanted and he must not undertake any fresh case until he has seen me."

"Very good, sir."

When his clerk had left the room Richardson began to run through the telephone messages received since the previous evening, marking most of them "F.P.", signifying "former papers to be attached." They would then go to the C.I.D. Registry and return to him a little later with bulky files tied up in bundles. He had scarcely finished his task when Constable Goodwin returned, holding one of the flimsies from the telephone room at the top of the building.

"What have you got there?" asked Richardson.

"A message from the chief constable of Surrey, sir."

Richardson read it. It was the request for help that he had expected for the shooting case at Marplesdon.

"Ask Inspector Dallas to come round."

Two minutes later a man of about thirty-five announced himself with a single sharp rap on the door.

"You wanted to see me, sir."

"Yes, Mr Dallas. I have here a telephone message from the C.C. of Surrey asking for our help in a murder case at Marplesdon. He is sending over Chief Inspector Vernon to explain the circumstances. You have nothing pressing on hand at the moment?"

"No sir."

'Well then, you'd better take on this case. Look out for Chief Inspector Vernon and go with him. You needn't trouble the chief inspector to come and see me unless he particularly wishes to. The case may turn out to be simpler than it appears in the newspaper report."

*

Next morning Richardson found at the top of the papers on his writing table a report with a green label marked "pressing" attached to it. He knew the handwriting as that of Detective Inspector Dallas.

"In accordance with instructions I met Chief Inspector Vernon on his arrival and we proceeded together to Scudamore Hall, owned by Mr Forge. It is a large house finished only a few weeks ago. On our way Mr Vernon gave me an account of the crime as far as he knew it. The body of the woman in evening dress had been discovered by a labourer named Henry Farnell on his way to work in the morning of December twentieth, Crooked Lane being on the direct line he would take from his cottage to his place of work. He informed the police and the body was carried into the schoolhouse at Marplesdon to await the inquest. It had been identified by Mr Forge as that of a young lady, Margaret Gask, a member of his house party at Scudamore Hall. She had been shot through the head, probably by a revolver bullet which had gone through the skull from left to right, but in spite of an exhaustive search no trace of the bullet could be discovered.

"Mr Forge, the owner of the Hall, was a war profiteer and had contrived to stick to his fortune. Nothing is known against him. I gathered that Mr Forge has a habit of picking up chance acquaintances in hotel bars. It was thus that he had first made the acquaintance of the murdered woman, Margaret Gask, in a Paris hotel. He speaks no French and when he was in difficulties in the reception room at the Hotel Terminus she volunteered her help, being quite qualified to act as an interpreter, though her intervention was not really necessary, since most of the staff speak English intelligibly. During his stay in Paris she acted as guide and he invited her to come over to England as a member of his house party at Scudamore Hall for Christmas. After a slight demur she consented. She had been his guest for only four days when her body was discovered shot through the head in the road known as Crooked Lane.

"On questioning the guests and staff at Scudamore Hall, Chief Inspector Vernon ascertained that the last person to see the deceased woman alive was a young man named Gerald Huskisson, of no occupation and known to be in financial straits. He also had met the woman in Paris and though he was believed to be in love with her he had had a serious quarrel with her—a fact that was known to other guests at the Hall.

"Mr Vernon also informed me that he had made a search of the premises and had discovered in a shed at a small distance from the ordinary garage an Austin Twelve car bearing the number P.J.C.4291. The chief inspector recognised the number as that of a car which was wanted in connection with serious injuries to a woman who had been knocked down by it near Kingston. The driver had accelerated without stopping to succour the injured woman. Mr Vernon took the usual steps to discover the owner and found that it belonged to a Mr Oborn, a guest at the Hall. When questioned at Police Headquarters he denied all knowledge of the accident and said that a dent on the fender had been caused by bad steering when entering the shed. The number of the car had been supplied by two witnesses who saw the accident.

"Arriving at Scudamore Hall the door was opened by a man dressed like a butler. I recognised this man as Alfred Curtis, alias Thomas Wilson, with Criminal Record Office number 2753. He has had five or six previous convictions, always for the same kind of offence—getting himself engaged as an indoor servant with a forged character and robbing members of the house party. He seemed much disconcerted at seeing me and without disclosing his identity I put discreet questions to Mr Forge about the butler's movements on the night of the murder. It had been a very foggy night and some of the invited guests had telephoned to say that they might arrive very late, owing to the fog. The butler had therefore had to sit up until past 3 A.M. to receive them. Thus he had a watertight alibi if Dr Treherne, who made the post-mortem, was correct in believing that the woman had been shot not later than midnight.

"The coroner intends to hold the inquest in the school-house at Marplesdon this afternoon at 2 P.M. and both Chief Inspector Vernon and I will be present. We think that it would be unwise to question any of the witnesses until they have given their evidence.

"ALBERT DALLAS, *Detective Inspector*."

Richardson finished reading the report and rang for his messenger.

"Ask Inspector Dallas to come, if he is in the building."

When Dallas presented himself Richardson said, "I've been reading your report. What impression did you form of the people you saw at Scudamore Hall?"

"Well, sir, besides that ex-convict mentioned in my report I saw only Mr Forge, the owner of the house. He was greatly upset by the occurrence and kept saying, 'This has been a lesson to me not to pick up chance acquaintances in a Paris hotel.'"

"Had he any explanation to offer as to why that young woman should have gone out at or after midnight in evening dress?"

"He thought she had gone out to keep a rendezvous with someone; he did not think it could be another member of the house party because the maid who waited on the murdered woman told him that a valuable mink coat was missing from her room and she must have been wearing it on such a cold night, yet her body was found with no wrap of any kind over her evening dress: the murderer had apparently stolen the coat."

"H'm! Then that fur coat may be a clue to her murderer."

"Yes sir, if it can be found, but Mr Vernon tells me that according to the maid it bore no distinguishing mark by which it could be identified; it had not even the name of the maker; the maid is positive about that because she had examined it carefully."

"Had Mr Forge nothing to tell you about the woman's friends or relations in France or in this country?"

"Nothing at all, sir. Mr Vernon has already written to the police judiciaire in Paris asking for full enquiry to be made about her, telling them the date when she was staying at the Hotel Terminus St Lazare. A search of her papers produced nothing of interest to the police."

"You say in your report that no trace of the bullet could be found in Crooked Lane. Were there any signs of a car having passed through?"

"Yes sir. I have been with Mr Vernon to the spot in Crooked Lane where the body was found and in spite of the ground being lightly frozen I could distinctly trace the wheel tracks of a light car which had broken through the frozen crust of mud. There is a gateway into a field a few yards from the spot and I could trace tracks of the car in the manoeuvre of turning in that gateway. There were no tracks nearer the house, but on the other side of the gate there were double tracks: the car must have returned in the direction from which it came. Since writing my report I have made enquiries at one or two cottages at the end of the lane. One woman said that she had heard a car passing in the direction of Crooked Lane and had seen through her window the glare of headlights as it returned."

"You say that one of the guests at Scudamore Hall had left his car in a shed and not in the proper garage. Have you enquired the reason for this?"

"No sir, not yet. I was waiting until after the inquest. That car is the one that I mentioned in my report as being suspected of having knocked down and gravely injured a woman."

"I see. Well, you will attend the inquest this afternoon and let me hear the result as soon as possible."

"Very good, sir."

Chapter Two

THE BREAKFAST TABLE at Scudamore Hall was set with only three places when the gong rang and the host, Walter Forge, struck a serio-comic attitude on entering the room and finding only Huskisson and Oborn present.

"Good Lord!" he said. "Is this what we're reduced to—three hungry men and no ladies? I hope that you have appetites; I'm as hungry as a hawk. What have we here?" he went on, going to the side table where four or five dishes were sputtering over spirit lamps. "The rule of the house is that everybody helps himself. Come along, you two, and make your choice."

When they had taken their seats Forge tried to lighten the gloom of his two guests by forced gaiety.

"This inquest this afternoon is the devil. I've never attended one before and I hear that the coroner is a grim bloke with a mouth set like a steel trap. I dunno what sort of figure I shall cut in a witness box. Have they summoned both of you?"

"Only me," said Huskisson; "I suppose because I was the last person in the house party to see her alive—poor girl."

"And I because she was staying in my house, I suppose. You've not had a summons?" he asked, turning to Oborn.

"No, thank God! And that's why I'm going to attack these sausages with an unimpaired appetite."

"Your turn will come when you're had before the beak for knocking down that woman," said Huskisson sourly.

"I never knocked her down," said Oborn in his pleasant voice. He was an upstanding and rather good-looking man in the early forties; well dressed, well groomed and easy mannered.

"Funny," said Huskisson, "that two people who saw the accident have come forward to give the number of your car."

"Both of them women. Have you ever met a woman yet who could remember the register number of a car? The fact that they both gave the same number is the proof that they concocted the story."

"I'm afraid that argument won't go down with the beaks and I'm told that the Kingston Bench gives short shrift to motorists."

Mr Forge's forced gaiety evaporated. "This is going to be the worst Christmas I've spent and I'd hoped that it was going to be the liveliest. I had counted so much on poor Margaret to keep things going."

Huskisson rose, leaving half his bacon and sausages uneaten. "I've just remembered that I've a telegram to answer if you'll excuse me," he said as he left the room.

He was a tall, thin, rather cadaverous-looking young man with lantern jaws.

"Our young friend seems to be taking this business very much to heart," said Oborn.

"He is; don't forget that he was fond of Margaret and I was beginning to think that she was fond of him, although they quarrelled."

"That won't sound very pretty when he's called into the box this afternoon," said Oborn. He changed his tone to an imitation of a coroner. "'You quarrelled with this lady on the evening before her death and you were the last person to see her alive. What was the quarrel about?' No, I don't wonder that he hasn't much appetite for breakfast."

"Oh, enough of this kind of talk," exclaimed Forge, whose nerves were frayed to breaking point. "Three or four of the people upstairs have sent messages that they are leaving this morning. Our party is practically broken up by this catastrophe. You won't be able to leave until this Kingston business is cleared up."

"No, unless they drag me off to a prison cell on the evidence of those two fools of women."

"Well, I feel like shutting up the house and packing off to Paris again. Her death would have upset me anyway, but to have been murdered in cold blood like this…Who the devil could it have been?"

Oborn helped himself to another sausage. Forge looked at him almost with repugnance. "You seem to take the thing lightly," he said.

"You forget I didn't know the lady."

"Didn't know her? Why, she told me that she was looking forward to meeting you again. In fact that was one of the reasons why I asked you to come down."

"Another feminine mistake. Oborn is not a very uncommon name."

"What is your first name?"

"Douglas."

"Oh no, that wasn't it. It was an ordinary name like Jim or Jack that she gave me—Jim, I'm sure it was."

"There you are," said Oborn, shrugging his shoulders. "If you want proof of my name I can show you my motor licence, my A.A. membership card and my passport. Those ought to be good enough."

"Have you got a second name?" asked Forge.

"I have, but it's a guilty secret I like to keep to myself. My godfathers and godmother conferred on me the name of Cadwallader and I've been trying to bury the name for the past forty years."

Forge was in no mood for flippancy. He pushed back his plate and went towards the door. "You can amuse yourself this morning, I suppose. I shall be busy."

"Righto! I've got letters to write and a lot of things to see to. Have I your permission to use your telephone for long-distance calls?"

"Of course; as many as you like."

Left to himself, Oborn picked up the morning paper and scanned the headlines. His attention was caught by a paragraph relating the facts of the Kingston accident and giving the date of the hearing. The butler slithered into the room unobtrusively, as all good butlers should. After shutting the door and looking round him he came forward and murmured, "Bad business, that accident."

"Yes, it was unfortunate, but these things will happen."

"It was a blasted silly thing to do. You'd better have stood your ground. Now, with your bolting like that there'll be a lot more publicity—just what we want to avoid."

"Don't you jump to conclusions, my friend: they're not healthy." Then, with a sudden change of tone due to the entrance of the footman, he said, "Yes, you're right; probably we're in for snow."

"Yes sir," responded the butler. "It promises to be quite a Christmas card sort of Christmas."

The morning was spent in the bustle of departures. All the guests were leaving except those whom the police had warned to remain within call. The inquest had been fixed for two o'clock.

Huskisson and Forge lunched early and drove off to the coroner's court together. The popular Press had already contrived to invest the proceedings with mystery; it is astonishing to see how many people can find time to attend any kind of public enquiry if it involves a mystery. The seats allotted to the public in the court were altogether insufficient for the number of people who sought admission, since the space available was much reduced by the presence of reporters from most of the newspapers, both morning and evening. A queue had had to be formed. To gain admission was an easy matter for Mr Forge and Huskisson, who had only to show their subpoenas. Huskisson was subjected to close scrutiny, for the rumour that he had been in love with the murdered woman had already been circulated.

The Surrey coroner was a strong man with a sound belief in the efficacy of police enquiries: he had already made up his mind to direct his jury to return an open verdict, which would leave the police a free hand in carrying out their enquiries. The first witness called was Henry Farnell. He described in laconic sentences how he was passing along Crooked Lane on his way to work when he came upon the body of the deceased lying on her side with her head towards the direction from which he was approaching. Seeing that the body showed no sign of life, he did not touch it but went to the police station to report what he had seen.

The next witness was Arthur Stove, a police constable who had been sent by his superintendent in charge of an ambulance stretcher to bring the body to the village schoolhouse. Judging from the fact that the woman was wearing evening dress, the superintendent surmised that she was one of the guests at Scudamore Hall and he sent the witness to the Hall to make enquiries. Mr Forge then came down to the schoolhouse and identified the body. The superintendent notified the coroner.

Hid you find any weapon, bullet or cartridge case on the spot?"

"No sir. I made a very careful search and found nothing."

"You found nothing that would give a clue to the identity of the murderer?"

"Nothing, sir."

The next witness was Dr Treherne, who had made the post-mortem examination. He testified that the woman was aged about twenty-seven or twenty-eight. The cause of death had been a bullet which traversed the brain and he judged from the state of the body that death had taken place not later than midnight.

"Could the wound have been self-inflicted?" asked the coroner.

"In my opinion, no. If that had been the case the weapon would have been found near the body; moreover, the direction of the shot would probably have been upward, whereas in fact it was horizontal."

"Had she been shot from behind?"

"No sir; the bullet entered on the right side of the head and emerged at about the same level on the left."

"Were there any signs of a struggle or bruising?"

"None at all."

The next witness was Walter Forge, who spoke of having identified the body as that of one of his guests at Scudamore Hall. He had met her in a hotel in Paris but he knew nothing whatever about her family or her history."

"Did any member of your household see her go out that night?"

"No one, but I have since learned from the maid who waited on her that her fur coat is missing."

"At what hour on that evening did you last see her?"

"As far as I can remember she left the bridge table when I did, at about ten o'clock. I was occupied after that in receiving other guests who had been delayed by the fog."

"Did anyone else leave the bridge table at the same time?"

"Yes; Mr Huskisson. We left one table and three new arrivals took our places."

Gerald Huskisson was the next witness. He was essentially what lawyers would call a bad witness in the impression he left on the jury. He hesitated before answering every question as if he feared committing himself by his answer and left the impression on the minds of all who heard him that he had something to hide.

"At what hour did you last see the deceased alive?"

"I suppose that it was about eleven."

"You left the bridge table together at ten o'clock?"

"Yes, to make room for other players."

"Did you spend approximately the next hour with her?"

"A good part of it."

"Where?"

"In the library."

"Was anyone else in the library at that time?"

"No."

"Did you have a quarrel?"

"I suppose you might call it a quarrel."

The coroner leaned forward. "What did you quarrel about?"

"That I must decline to say. It was an entirely private matter."

The coroner's lower jaw advanced half an inch. He was not accustomed to evasive replies to his questions. After all, the coroner's court, as he knew, was the oldest in the kingdom. He repeated his question. "What —did—you—quarrel—about?"

"I—decline—to—say."

"Very well, then the jury will form their own conclusions. How long had you known Miss Gask?"

"I first met her in Paris about six months ago."

"Were you on very friendly terms with her?"

"Y-e-s; quite friendly."

"Did you see much of her?"

"A good deal."

"Which of you left the library first on that night?"

Huskisson hesitated, as if trying to remember. "I think I did."

"What did you do then?"

"I went to bed."

"You didn't join any of the other guests?"

"No."

"And you left this young woman alone in the library?"

"I did."

"And never saw her again alive?"

"No."

The coroner considered for a moment and then began his summing up. He said that the medical evidence left no doubt at all it had been a case of murder and not suicide. He pointed out that so far no weapon had been found and that there was no evidence against any particular member of the house party at Scudamore Hall. "The police are pursuing their enquiries and you may safely leave the question of the perpetrator of this crime to them. My advice to you is to find a verdict of wilful murder by some person unknown."

Heads went together on the jury benches and after less than three minutes exchange of views the foreman stood up and returned a verdict of wilful murder by some person unknown.

Chapter Three

ON THE following morning Richardson found lying on his table a typewritten report bearing the signature "Albert Dallas, Detective Inspector."

"SIR,

"In accordance with your instructions I attended the inquest at Marplesdon and was present when the jury returned an open verdict of 'murder by some person or persons unknown', leaving the police a free hand. The evidence of the witnesses called by the coroner threw no further light upon the case other than what I have already reported. The witness Huskisson was unsatisfactory. He gave his evidence with reluctance and it was clear both to the coroner and myself that he was keeping something back. As to the cause of the quarrel between him and the murdered woman, he refused any information and I formed the opinion from his manner and his reluctance that it was not a mere lovers' quarrel. His story was that he left the deceased in the library at 11 P.M. and went straight to bed. In the interviews that I had later with members of the household I found nothing either to confirm or to disprove his statement. The most useful informant was Mary Hooper, the parlour-maid who waited on the lady guests. Her statement was as follows:

"'Miss Gask was a very lively young lady, not reserved like many of them are. She chatted with me freely and told me how much she liked living in Paris. She said she wondered why English girls like myself did not get jobs there so as to learn the language, because they would command higher wages if they spoke French. It was a great shock to me when I heard of her death, because she had promised to give me a lot more information about getting a job in Paris. It is my belief that she must have been wearing her mink coat on the night she was shot. I had often admired it and one day I took it down from the hanger to look for the maker's name, but it had no distinguishing mark of any kind. When I heard that her body had been found lying in a lane on a bitterly cold night with only an evening dress on I went straight to the cupboard to look for her coat. It was not there. She must have had it on when she went out. I helped her to dress for dinner that night and I never saw her alive again.'

"My next interview was with the butler, Alfred Curtis, alias Tommy Wilson. He said, 'I saw that you had recognised me, sir, but I hope you won't give me away just when I'm making good.' I said that he'd no reason to fear that provided that he was really making good, but that his record showed that he had had more than one chance since his first release and had abused them all. He assured me that this time I need have no reason to fear. As to the murder, he said that he could throw no light upon it at all. Guests were arriving at all hours that night and he was kept busy answering the telephone, carrying sandwiches upstairs, right up to three in the morning. He did not see any lady go out but the hall door remained unlocked practically all night. From what I know of this man in the past I should attach no importance to anything he said.

"I ought to mention that Mr Forge, the owner of the house, came to me and said, 'I've been thinking over things and there is one small matter which I think I ought to tell you. When Miss Margaret Gask arrived she asked me the names of my other guests. I told her that among them a Mr Oborn had been asked but had not then accepted. She said, "Oh, I hope he will; I like Jim Oborn: he's such good company." On the day of the inquest Oborn told me emphatically that he had never met her and his Christian name was Douglas.'

"I asked Mr Forge what happened when Oborn and Miss Gask met at Scudamore Hall but he could not remember. He had assumed that they knew one another.

"I asked Mr Forge where and when he first met Mr Oborn and he replied that he had met him in a London hotel quite recently.

"I then asked to see Mr Oborn and after a few introductory questions I asked him when he had first met Miss Gask, the murdered woman. He showed surprise at my question and said, 'I first met her at this house five minutes before dinner on the evening of my arrival.'

"'Who introduced you?' I asked.

"'No one. It was a free and easy party and no introductions were necessary.'

"I saw Mr Huskisson in private in the library and asked him point-blank where he had first met the murdered woman. He said, 'In Paris,' and then a little later he contradicted this statement by saying, 'When I first met Miss Gask in Nice...' I called his attention to the discrepancy in his previous statement and he seemed to be confused. 'Did I say Nice? I meant Paris.'"

Richardson took up his blue pencil and underscored the names "Nice" and "Paris." Then he continued to read.

"I learned from Mr Forge that as soon as his present guests have left him he intends to shut up the house and return to Paris. He will leave his Paris address with me before he goes. Mr Oborn is remaining as a guest at Scudamore Hall until after the Kingston summons for dangerous driving has been disposed of. (In my last report you will remember I gave details of this accident.) The butler, Alfred Curtis, C.R.O. number 2753, has still to report to the police and therefore his address can always be ascertained. Gerald Huskisson has given me the address of his flat in Richmond.

"No suspicion attaches to any of these people; the probability is that the deceased woman went out to keep an appointment with someone who arrived in a car. Her bedroom at Scudamore Hall, which has remained locked since her death, was searched by me today. This had already been done by Chief Inspector Vernon and a member of his staff. Her English bankbook showed a balance of £312.11.6. and in her purse there were five one-pound notes, thirteen shillings in silver and fourpence-half-penny in coppers. Her chequebook showed that she had drawn out five pounds on the eve of her visit to Scudamore Hall. She had also a small balance at the Paris branch of the Westminster Bank. Her wardrobe appeared to be fashionable and costly as far as I could judge. Her personal letters had been taken away by Mr Vernon, who was making enquiry into the identity of the writers: three of them were ardent letters from admirers, but none of them made a rendezvous for the night of her death.

"Mr Vernon has not yet received any reply from Paris.

"ALBERT DALLAS, *Detective Inspector*."

Richardson marked the paper "further report", threw it into the registry basket and took up the papers relating to another case marked "pressing."

*

During that afternoon fingers tapped on Richardson's door and the tap was followed by the entry of Inspector Dallas.

"I'm sorry to interrupt you, sir, but information has just been given me bearing on that case at Scudamore Hall in Surrey and I think that you ought to know it. This morning Chief Inspector Vernon was rung up by Mr Forge and was asked to come round without delay. I was in his office at the time so he asked me to go with him. We found Mr Forge in a state of great agitation. He told us that he had just discovered the loss of a very valuable uncut emerald which he kept in a locked drawer in his bureau. We asked him when he had last seen it. He said that it was on the evening before Miss Gask's body was found in Crooked Lane. He had shown it to her and other ladies of the party; he then replaced it in the drawer. He showed me the key of this drawer on a key ring in his pocket but said that though his instinct was always to keep the drawer locked he could not say positively that he had locked it on that occasion."

"Ah!" sighed Richardson. "That's the type of man that makes things easy for criminals. Has Mr Forge mentioned his loss to any of his guests?"

"No sir; I found that he was reluctant to do this and I told him that in my view it would not help the course of justice if he did. Mr Vernon and I went over the bureau with camel-hair brush and powdered chalk but such fingerprints as we disclosed were blurred and quite useless for identification purposes."

Richardson laughed shortly. "If you were writing detective fiction, Mr Dallas, no fingerprint would ever be blurred; they would always be made with the care necessary to assist police investigations."

"Indeed, sir? I never read detective fiction."

"Wise man. Real detective work doesn't leave much room for fiction. You are going to have your hands full over this case, I'm afraid. Half London and Paris seem to have been in and out of Scudamore Hall about that time. Of course there's the ex-convict butler."

"Yes sir, but I think we may rule him out. He knows on which side his bread is buttered and with C.I.D. men from the Yard fussing round he'll not take risks."

"Have you obtained a list of Mr Forge's guests at the Hall—I mean the guests who left in consequence of the murder?"

"Yes sir, and their addresses: that is what I am now going into."

"Was he able to give you a good description of the emerald?"

"Only as regards the size and weight."

"And have you circulated this in the pawnbrokers' list?"

"Yes sir; I've just sent that out to all pawnbrokers but I'm afraid this emerald may be in the hands of a receiver and we know how difficult it is to bring one of those fellows to justice."

"Of course Mr Forge had no suspicion of any of his guests. Were they all chance acquaintances picked up in hotels?"

"Not all of them, sir. I've got one couple on this list who seem to be in the habit of living in hotels or on their friends. They are Mr and Mrs Ermine. Nothing is known against them in the Criminal Record Office and they may turn out to be beyond reproach. The other people on the list have all settled addresses and I should think that they are beyond suspicion."

"Has Mr Vernon received any information from Paris about the murdered woman?"

"Yes sir. The information came this morning that she had lived in France for the last five years and that nothing is known against her. I've been round to the Passport Office and have seen the chief officer, who gave me the names of the two persons who recommended her when she took out the passport five years ago. Unfortunately both these persons are dead. They were men of position—a solicitor and a doctor both in considerable practice. Probably she knew them professionally."

"Have you found out how she derived her income?"

"Not yet, sir. Her bankers say that she brought in sums of money in notes from time to time and had them credited to her current account. She seemed to have spent her time between France and England. There was only one cheque for three hundred pounds signed by Mr Forge. When asked about this he said that it was a loan to Miss Gask to enable her to start a dressmaking business."

"Why should Mr Forge have lent this woman three hundred pounds?" said Richardson half to himself.

"From facts I have gathered I should think that Miss Gask was a young woman who lived on her wits and reaped little harvests from men of the type of Mr Forge."

"Then in that case she may have picked up a number of shady acquaintances."

"Yes sir, that is what I mean."

"I noticed in your first report that you mentioned Huskisson as a young man in financial straits. Have you made any further enquiries about him?"

"Yes sir. He lives with his widowed mother, who has a small pension as the widow of a colonel. In business he has been more sinned against than sinning. He went into partnership with a man who had started on the road downhill. This man got away with Huskisson's share of the capital and left him stranded. Since then he has secured odd jobs as salesman for second-hand cars."

"He was supposed to be in love with the dead woman, Miss Gask. Have you got any further details about that side of the story?"

"The only details I could get came from Mr Forge, who is a garrulous type of man and apt to embroider what he knows with details drawn from conjecture. On one point Mr Forge was emphatic. He said that the dead woman was very good looking and fascinating and Huskisson was extremely jealous if he saw her being civil to other men. He was even jealous of Mr Forge himself, who was his host."

"I see from your report that there had been a quarrel between Huskisson and this woman. Who knew about this quarrel?"

"The report came originally from one of the servants but it was confirmed by Mr Forge. According to the servant who first reported the quarrel she went into the library during the morning to fetch Mr Huskisson, who was wanted on the telephone, and came upon him and the dead woman apparently struggling together. Neither heard her approach and as far as she could judge Huskisson was trying to wrest something from Miss Gask's hand by force. The struggle was quite silent."

"Was this woman called as a witness at the inquest?"

"No sir; as it seemed likely to become a police case of some importance, Chief Inspector Vernon and I decided against giving the incident publicity."

"What was Mr Forge's account of the quarrel?"

"Miss Gask herself had told him that she and Gerald Huskisson had had a quarrel during the morning about a letter she had received. She had refused to show it to him."

"Then it may have been quite unimportant."

"Yes sir; it may, but the servant told me that if it had been a letter she would have seen the paper. This was something solid that Miss Gask was holding in her clenched hand."

"H'm. We all know the weakness servants have for importing cheap drama into everything that goes on in the household upstairs."

"Yes sir; I'm taking that into account."

Chapter Four

SOON AFTER BREAKFAST on the day following the inquest on Margaret Gask a police officer called at Scudamore Hall and asked for Mr Oborn, who went down to the front door to see him. A few minutes later Oborn sought out his host and showed him a blue paper.

"Look at this," he said.

"A summons? For dangerous driving? Lucky for you the woman isn't dead."

"Why lucky for me? I've already told you that I never hit a woman or caused an accident."

"Then you'll have a job to prove it. That reminds me of a question I meant to ask you. What made you put your car into a shed instead of the garage?"

"Well, there was no one about and I didn't want to give trouble. The fog was pretty thick and I shoved the car into the first empty shelter I could find. The next morning your garage man told me that he'd been attending to the boiler house when I came in. The car's in the garage now."

"What beats me is why you took four hours and a half to get here from Kingston, which is only eight miles away. That woman was knocked down at three o'clock and you arrived at 7.30 P.M."

"I can see that you have swallowed the story of those two women. Why don't you come along with me to the court and hear the proceedings. I can promise you quite an amusing time."

Forge showed his annoyance by his tone. "Why can't you give me a straightforward explanation if you've got one?"

"Oh, I'm saving that up for the court. I always like to make the police look foolish if I can. Besides, they should have served this summons last night. I'll have to take my car and go straight away if I'm to be in time. Are you sure I can't give you a lift?"

"No thanks," said Forge shortly. "I shall hear all about it soon enough."

"You resent the notoriety Scudamore Hall is getting and I don't blame you. I should feel just the same in your place."

Forge watched him from the front door and saw him enter the garage, then on a sudden impulse he decided that he would like to hear the proceedings, though not in the company of the man most concerned. He entered the library in quest of Huskisson, who was immersed in a newspaper.

"Your newspaper can wait, my friend. Why not drive over with me to Kingston police court and hear how Oborn conducts himself from the dock."

"What? Is he in trouble?"

"Yes; he's got a summons for dangerous driving when that woman was knocked down. I'm curious to hear how he will lie his way out of it."

Huskisson threw down his paper and said, "When do we start? We seem to be getting quite a lot of police attention these days."

"We do," agreed Forge gloomily. "A good deal more than I like. Do you drive?"

"Rather—any kind of car. You forget that it's my job."

"Good; then we needn't take Strong with us."

He watched Huskisson examine the water in the radiator and start up the engine, then he took his place beside him in the car. There were none of the delicacies about Forge. They had scarcely reached the public road before he blurted out, "Do you like that fellow Oborn?" It might have been more delicately put by a host speaking of a guest but Huskisson had his answer ready.

"I don't know him well enough to say but I can see that you haven't taken to him."

"You never spoke a truer word. I haven't taken to him. I was wondering whether he had the same effect upon others."

"Well, if you won't think the question impertinent, why did you ask him here at all?"

"You know how it is when one's knocking about in hotels; one meets people and if they're decent folk one asks them to stay when one has a house of one's own. I wanted to fill the house for Christmas. You knew poor Margaret quite well; did you ever hear her mention Oborn's name?"

"Never."

"That's curious. She told me that she knew him and he swears that she never met him before."

"Another person of the same name, probably."

"That's the explanation he gave when I tackled him but Oborn is not a common name in my experience…If it had been Osborn now…But here we are. That's the police court."

There was only a sparse attendance in the public benches in the courthouse. When they entered the three magistrates sitting on the bench were disposing of two vagrants charged with hawking without a licence; these were wretched specimens of humanity and very dirty. Oborn was sitting on the front bench of the space reserved for the public. The constable acting as officer of the court called his name and ushered him into the dock. The solicitor acting as prosecutor engaged in a private colloquy with the chairman of the three magistrates sitting above him. It was his duty to keep them straight.

"The defendant is charged with dangerous driving at 3 P.M. on the nineteenth. He failed to stop at a pedestrian crossing, knocked down a woman and drove on without stopping to render aid. Happily the woman was not fatally injured. If she had been killed this man would have been charged with manslaughter."

"What have you to say?" enquired the presiding magistrate sternly.

"I have nothing to say," smiled the prisoner, "because I wasn't there."

The prosecuting solicitor turned to the magistrate.

"I have two witnesses who saw the accident, your worships." Then, turning to Oborn, he asked, "Is your car number P.J.C.4291?"

"It is."

"Were you driving it on the nineteenth?"

"I was, but not in Kingston."

The presiding magistrate put a question. "Have the witnesses identified this man as the driver?"

"Yes, your worships, they identified him outside the court a few minutes ago."

"Do you mean that they picked him out from a number of men in the ordinary course of police identification?"

The clerk consulted a police sergeant. "I understand that they did not pick him out from a line of men, which is the ordinary procedure for an identification parade, your worships; they merely indicated that he was the man who had been driving the car."

"Then if he can prove that he was not on the spot at the time of the accident it would be a case of mistaken identity. You had better call your witnesses."

"Ellen Wheeler," called the sergeant.

The name was repeated by an officer outside the court. A little woman with "charwoman" written all over her came bustling in and took her stand in the witness box.

"Take the book in your right hand," said the sergeant, "and swear that you will tell the truth, the whole truth and nothing but the truth, so help you God."

The little lady did as she was bidden. Her evidence was short and to the point. "It was this way, your worship: me and the lady who was knocked down was standing at the Belisha crossing waiting for a chance to slip over. The lady stepped off into the road, the car knocked her over and drove on without stopping. I shouted after him, 'You unfeeling swine,' and I took his number. It was P.J.C.4291."

Oborn cross-examined her. "You say you identified me as the driver."

"Yes."

"Was I driving fast?"

"You was driving like the wind."

"But not so fast that you couldn't take my number."

"Nah; I took that all right."

"Did you write it down?"

"No, I kept it in my 'ead."

"What a memory you must have to carry the figures in your head."

"I wasn't the only one. That other lady that's here took the number too."

The woman she referred to was a working woman of the same class. She confirmed Ellen Wheeler's evidence but when Oborn pressed her to say whether it was she or Mrs Wheeler who remembered the car's number she became confused. This did not prevent her from becoming impudent when asked which of the two had made up the story which both were pledged to tell.

"You think yourself very clever, don't you, putting me a question like that?"

"But you haven't answered the question."

She tossed her head. "No, and I ain't going to."

The presiding magistrate addressed Oborn. "It would be strange if either woman had invented a number which is that of your car."

"And yet that must have happened, your worship," said Oborn, pulling a paper from his pocket. "This is a certificate from an A.A. scout stationed near Wakefield, testifying that I, driving my car, number P.J.C.4291, stopped at three o'clock on that day to ask him whether he could supply me with a tin of petrol. Your worship will see that it was signed in the presence of a police inspector and therefore I could not have been in Surrey and Yorkshire at the same hour."

The presiding magistrate examined the paper and passed it to his colleagues.

"What do you say to that?" he asked the police inspector.

"If your worship will adjourn the case I have no doubt that the matter can be cleared up."

"I object to any adjournment," said Oborn.

The presiding magistrate showed impatience. He addressed Oborn first. "You have wasted the time of the Court. If you had produced this certificate to the police in the first instance the case would never have been called."

"I told the police officer who first questioned me that I was not in Kingston that day and as he didn't believe me I obtained this certificate. If I hadn't wanted petrol I might never have been able to prove my innocence." The chairman passed a slip of paper to his colleagues and when they nodded assent he pronounced the charge to have been dismissed.

Forge and Huskisson got into their car without waiting for Oborn and set out for home. Forge was the first to speak.

"I don't know what you think, but I consider that it was damned offhand of Oborn to keep all this up his sleeve when he was staying in my house. Why couldn't he have told us about his defence?"

"It seems to amuse him to get a rise out of the police."

"Oh, the police are quite able to look after themselves. What I object to is his taking a rise out of me."

"Yes, it's a poor sort of humour to play this kind of joke on one's host. I've been wondering if you've really decided to shut up the house and go abroad again. If so you mustn't think of me. I'll make other plans."

"Well, as a matter of fact something else has happened to keep me here. I haven't told anyone yet except the police, but I'd like to tell you..."

Huskisson broke in. "Please don't tell me any secrets. I'd rather not know them."

Forge looked rather disconcerted. "I was going to confide in you because I hate keeping things to myself and I'm in a hole. Still, if you don't want to hear it..."

"I'm sorry to seem unsympathetic—the fact of the matter is I have a lot of troubles of my own just now. If you've confided your troubles to the police, especially if you've told them to Inspector Dallas, you can be more easy in your mind than if you confided in me."

"You think Dallas is a live wire?"

"From what I've seen of him I should say that he is. You've only to look at him. There's bulldog tenacity written all over his face."

"Yes, I shouldn't like to get on the wrong side of him, I confess."

They arrived at the house and found Oborn there before them. He had handed his car over to the garage man and came towards them as they drove in.

"I feel I owe you an apology, Mr Forge," he said in his pleasant voice.

"What for?"

"For not having told you in advance about the little surprise I had prepared for the police."

"I couldn't understand why you didn't tell the police what you told the Court in the very beginning. You must remember that they have a very difficult part to play and after all they are only doing their duty."

"I'm afraid I belong to the other school. I think that a great part of their evidence against motorists is concocted and they need showing up. That's why I took no one into my confidence about the line of my defence."

Forge was mollified. "Oh well, you've had your joke and no one begrudges you, except perhaps the men in blue. I've just been telling Huskisson that I shan't go abroad after all and I hope that you two fellows will stay with me and help me over what fools call the festive season."

"I'm going to try to make it a festive season if you really want me to stay," said Oborn.

Huskisson grinned. "I'm going to stay until you kick me out," he said.

Chapter Five

DALLAS' NEXT REPORT, dated two days later, was read by Richardson with great care and with a free use of his blue pencil.

"In accordance with your instructions I have interviewed all the persons who were staying at Scudamore Hall at the time of the murder of Margaret Gask. Inspector Vernon was present with me at every interview."

(There followed a list of the guests and a statement that no suspicion could attach to any of them of having known Margaret Gask before they met her at Scudamore Hall.)

"Enquiries about the writers of the letters found in her room showed no grounds for doubt except in the single case of a letter attached to this report from one Arthur Graves. This man has been known to visit from time to time the house of a man, a registered moneylender, suspected of receiving stolen property at 49, Blenheim Road, Kingston-on-Thames. We interviewed this man Arthur Graves and with his consent searched his premises: nothing incriminating was found. He made the following statement to us and signed it in our presence.

"'I met Margaret Gask in Paris about six months ago. I had been over there on business.' (Richardson underscored the sentence with his blue pencil. He guessed the kind of business that Arthur Graves would be transacting on the other side of the Channel.) 'She told me that she was employed as a mannequin for Monsieur Henri in the Rue Royale. A few weeks ago I received a letter from her saying that she had left her employment and was trying to raise capital for starting a dressmaking business in England employing only British workwomen. She asked me whether I knew anyone who would be willing to advance the necessary capital. I haven't kept her letter but the one from me that you have was my answer to it.'"

Richardson broke off to read the letter which was attached to the report.

"DEAR MARGARET,

"I wish you luck in your new venture, but I know of no one who could be milked for the necessary funds. Drop me a line when you come over and we'll feed together somewhere.

"Yours,

"ARTHUR GRAVES"

Richardson resumed his reading of the report.

"This man declared, and we have no reason to doubt his statement, that he had not seen or made an appointment with Margaret Gask since her arrival in England. We questioned him about his relations with Hyam Fredman (the suspected receiver) and he stated without hesitation that Fredman was a moneylender and that he had gone to see him about a loan. Although Graves showed no discomposure on being questioned we feel some doubt as to the truth of this last statement and we decided to interview Hyam Fredman. His address proved to be an office building but his room was locked and we could get no answer. The lift boy said that Mr Fredman had not been there for several days and that his clerk could not understand the cause of his absence. The lift boy was able to supply us with the address of the clerk and we called at his house. It was a small house in a side street in Kingston; the young man was at home and made the following statement:

"'My name is Thomas Barker and I am twenty-four years old. I have been employed by Mr Fredman for six months and I have never known him take a holiday until the nineteenth of this month. Then he told me that he had an all-night journey to take and wouldn't be at the office until the afternoon of the twentieth, so I could have the morning off. He left the office that evening and I've never seen him since.'

"We then asked him whether Mr Fredman received clients at his office or called upon them at their homes. He said that his employer was very secretive and told him nothing but he believed that he called on a few personally. We asked the clerk for the key of the office and he said that he was never entrusted with the key; that Fredman was always in his office before he arrived each morning and was there at three o'clock in the afternoon when he returned from lunch; that he himself went off at six, leaving his employer in the office. He further explained that Mr Fredman left the office every morning punctually at eleven; that he himself had to stay until one-thirty when he pulled the door to behind him and it locked automatically.

"For a man of Mr Fredman's type from eleven till three seemed to be an unduly long luncheon hour. We returned to the office and asked for the caretaker. As we expected he was in possession of a master key. We took him upstairs with us in order that he might see what steps we took in searching the room. We found the room tidy but dusty; it had not been occupied for five days; the books appeared to be well kept; the safe was locked and we left it as it was. Among the letters we found an envelope that had been addressed to Mr Hyam Fredman, 10, Dover Street, Twickenham. We visited this address and found it to be an antique shop, but the shutters were on the window and a neighbour told us that Mr Fredman had not been there for several days. Generally speaking, he opened the shop just after eleven and closed it again before three and opened it again in the evening. Fearing that the man might have died suddenly, we took a locksmith to the shop; the lock was picked and we went in, shutting the door behind us. The floor of the shop was covered with ornaments of various kinds and clearly the owner was not dealing only in second-hand furniture. Among the objects was a candelabra which was recognised by Mr Vernon as one circulated in police informations a few days ago as having been stolen. This confirmed

Mr Vernon's suspicion that Fredman was a receiver. The room behind the shop was also a sort of museum of artistic objects but we did not stop to examine them then. A narrow staircase led upstairs; there were two rooms. The room we first entered was a kitchen with a gas stove; the room beyond that was a bedroom: they were tidy but dusty, like everything else. The front room was a living room and here we found the body of a man of about fifty lying on the floor; there were stains of dried blood which apparently had come from the head. An examination of the body showed that it had been shot through the head. We sent for the police surgeon and an ambulance and the body was removed to the mortuary. The medical report by the police surgeon, Dr Smithers, will follow as soon as it is received.

"I have not visited Scudamore Hall today, but I sent Sergeant Wilkins to the Kingston police court to hear the proceedings against Douglas Oborn for dangerous driving. His report is attached.

"ALBERT DALLAS, *Detective Inspector*."

The report of Detective Sergeant Wilkins was terse. It stated that Douglas Oborn had been acquitted on the charge of dangerous driving; he had proved an alibi and therefore it must have been a case of mistaken identity.

Richardson confessed to himself that of all the cases that were coming before him at this moment, this murder of one of the guests at Scudamore Hall was the most intriguing. He touched his bell and told his messenger to waylay Detective Inspector Dallas when he came in and bring him to his room.

"I shall not leave the office before I have seen him."

"Very good, sir; I'll tell him."

It was past seven when Dallas tapped on his chief's door.

"Come in," called Richardson. "You seem to have had a busy day."

"Yes sir, I have." His usual calm self-possession appeared to have been shaken.

"Have you any fresh news to report about that Marplesdon case?"

"Yes sir; we have found Mr Forge's missing emerald."

"Good Lord! Found it where?"

"On the body of that suspected receiver, Hyam Fredman, about whom I reported this morning. The first search of the body had disclosed nothing but in feeling the clothing carefully over we felt some hard object and found on the inside of the vest another pocket that had been added to the garment, not by a tailor, but by a clumsy amateur. In this secret pocket we found the missing emerald."

"Has Mr Forge identified it?"

"Yes sir; he had already given us the weight and the approximate size and the jewel conformed with his description."

"That rascally butler was in it, I suppose."

"Well, sir, I think that there are more complications than that. As you will remember, Fredman's clerk told me that he left home on the nineteenth and said something about a night journey. The nineteenth was of course the night of the murder and we formed the impression on finding that emerald that the two were connected in some way. If it was his intention to visit Crooked Lane that night to receive the emerald from the thief he must have had a car, so we specialised on finding out whether this was so and we discovered that he had a car—an ancient, broken-down-looking vehicle which he kept in a small garage near the shop. We searched this car and at the bottom of the pocket on the door beside the driver's seat we found this, sir." With great care Dallas drew an envelope from his pocket and took out of it a rough manuscript plan which he unfolded and laid before Richardson. It indicated Scudamore Hall, the road over Marplesdon Common and Crooked Lane with a line of dots and arrows marking the route.

"You think that the dead woman was the thief and that she had made an appointment with this man?"

"That seems to be a probable explanation, sir," said Dallas cautiously.

"Do you suggest that he committed the murder and then killed himself in his own house?"

"That seems a feasible explanation; we found a revolver with two chambers empty, on the floor beside the body. Doctor Smithers will let us have his report as soon as he has consulted the medical expert employed by the Home Office in such cases."

"Probably the expert's report will go far towards clearing up this case altogether for you."

"Personally, I am inclined to think that there is a good deal of work before us, sir."

"You don't accept the prima facie evidence then?"

"Not altogether, sir. There is still the mystery of the missing fur coat; I myself searched the shop and the rooms upstairs and it wasn't there."

"Did you find out from the garage people at what hour Fredman brought his car back?"

"Yes sir; he brought it back on the morning of the twentieth about ten o'clock."

"Then he had it out all night?"

"Yes sir, as far as we've been able to ascertain."

"You say that the revolver was lying on the floor near the body and was not grasped in the hand."

"It was eight and a half inches from the right hand, sir."

"In my opinion that would not point to suicide. A very important and in fact almost certain proof of suicide is the manner in which the corpse retains the weapon in his clenched fist.

All sorts of experiments have been made on persons just dead by pressing objects into their hands and these have proved that they cannot continue grasping such objects with the convulsive grip of a person who was holding the object in his hand during life and in the death agony, unless, of course, the weapon was placed in the hand of a dying victim. So, subject to the opinion of the Home Office expert, I think it is clear that Hyam Fredman was murdered."

"I think to, too, sir, and we shall work on those lines."

"Then let me hear the doctor's report as soon as it comes in."

Chapter Six

No ONE would have thought that tragedy was hanging over the little party of three who sat in the dining room at Scudamore Hall on Christmas Eve, albeit they had attended the funeral of Margaret Gask that very morning. Huskisson, it was true, was still plunged in gloom but Oborn was a host in himself. As if to make up for having sprung the surprise of his alibi upon them without telling them beforehand, he entertained his two companions with amusing stories throughout the meal. Forge seemed to forget his distaste for the man. No one touched on the topic of Margaret Gask's death but Oborn in his triumph at the police court could not resist the temptation to make slighting references to the police. Forge at once took up the cudgels on their behalf.

"They've got pretty good men in the metropolitan police," he said.

"And plenty of dunderheads, too—fellows who go off the deep end on the slightest provocation. Look at that fellow—Dallas, I think he calls himself; there's a deep-ender for you..."

Forge turned upon him. "Don't start talking about Inspector Dallas disparagingly..."

"Why? Has he been making good behind my back?"

"Well, I'll tell you something and you can judge for yourselves. Now we are free from interruption by the servants let me say that I've recovered a very valuable thing that was pinched by someone in the house no longer ago than three or four days and this was done entirely by Dallas. You remember that uncut emerald I showed you all? Well, to the best of my belief I locked it up in the drawer, meaning to put it back in the safe as soon as I had a moment to spare, but when I went to the drawer I found that it had disappeared and yet I could swear that I locked it up."

"You mean that the lock on the drawer was picked?" asked Huskisson.

"It must have been."

"You don't suspect any of your guests, I hope?" asked Oborn with a grin.

Forge dismissed the joke with a gesture. "You must keep this entirely to yourselves. Obviously the theft must have been committed by someone in the house and all my servants are more or less new. The police are looking up the characters they brought with them but have warned me not to alarm them and so I hope you will both keep your mouths shut about the theft."

The butler came in and, addressing Forge, said, "I'm sorry to disturb you, sir, but there's a lady on the telephone asking for Miss Gask."

"Did you tell her what had happened?" asked Forge.

"No sir; I said that I would call you to speak to the lady."

Forge made a gesture of resignation. "You'll excuse me," he said to his guests as he went out to the instrument in the hall.

He took up the receiver and listened to a voice with a strong foreign accent.

"Who is speaking?" he asked.

"Mademoiselle Coulon. I wish to speak to Miss Gask; she told me she would be there, so will you call her, please."

Forge clasped and unclasped the fingers of his free hand, wondering how one broke bad news gently. Through his brain—never of the brightest—there flashed the thought that to temporise would only put off the evil day and might possibly involve him in a suspicion of foul play. He must temporise, nevertheless. "I'm sorry to tell you that there has been an accident."

The voice at the other end rose almost to a scream. "An accident to Margaret? Is she hurt very badly, yes?"

"Yes, very badly."

"Oh, where is she? I must go to see her at once."

"I'm afraid it's too late." Forge quickly abandoned all hope of temporising. It was safer to blurt out the truth. "The fact is we attended her funeral this morning." There was a silence at the other end of the wire; Forge began to fear that the speaker had collapsed in a faint with the instrument in her hand. At last came the words in a faint voice: "Margaret dead: it is not possible; and so suddenly. Then what am I to do? I come from arriving in London just half an hour ago. Margaret wrote to me that her friends would be pleased if I came to stay with them, so I came, but if she is dead..."

The voice was a pleasant one, the accent that of an educated woman; Forge forgot his resolution never again to invite to his house chance acquaintances—and if this lady at the other end of the wire was not a chance acquaintance what was she? But he could not keep her waiting.

"Come all the same," he said, "and I can tell you all about it when you come."

"But how shall I get there?"

"Where are you now?"

"I am speaking from Waterloo Station."

"Nothing could be better. Ask for the platform for the next train to Kingston and I will send the car to meet you there. The chauffeur will be told to ask for Mademoiselle Coulon."

"But that sounds very easy. I ask for Kingston, is it not so? And you will tell your chauffeur to look for a lady all in dark blue with a green wing in her hat and I will tell him my name."

It is always pleasant to play the part of a knight-errant and Forge returned to his guests with the glow still upon him. He explained to them what had happened.

"Mademoiselle Coulon!" exclaimed Huskisson with a note of pleasure in his voice. "Why, that must be Pauline Coulon."

"You know her then?" asked Forge.

"I do and she's a very charming person."

"She must be," agreed Oborn, "for do you know that she's lifted the atmosphere of gloom from your brow for the first time since I met you."

"Perhaps you would go in the car to meet her at Kingston, as you know her," said Forge; "and, by the way, the car ought to be starting soon: the trains run pretty often."

"Have you told her what has happened?" asked Huskisson.

"I told her that poor Margaret Gask was dead but I did not say how she met her death."

"Oh, then I suppose that will be my pleasant job," observed Huskisson, on whom a deeper gloom had descended. "However, I'll be off."

"I don't envy him his job," said Oborn when Huskisson had shut the door behind him.

"No more do I, but it'll be easier for him than it would have been for us who have never met the lady."

"Do you think you acted wisely in inviting her to come to a house where her friend has just been murdered?"

"What else could I do? She had been invited to this house by poor Margaret and I couldn't leave her stranded without a friend in London. After all, we ought to be able between us to make her forget the tragedy."

"I hope she won't mind there being no hostess."

"Well, you see I've got no female relations. Margaret, poor girl, was to have acted as hostess. I would have asked Huskisson's mother to come and stay for Christmas but it seems that she has already accepted an invitation to go to some friends in Scotland. If you'll excuse me I think I'll see the housekeeper myself about a room for Mademoiselle."

As soon as the door had closed behind Forge, Oborn rang the bell. It was answered by the butler, who, seeing that Oborn was alone, closed the door behind him.

"I'm glad you answered the bell. Tell me quickly. Did you ever hear Margaret speak of a French friend called Pauline Coulon?"

"Never," said the butler without hesitation.

"Good. That's all I wanted to know. Clear out now before Forge comes back."

A minute later Forge returned with an expression of satisfaction on his face.

"We must make this lady comfortable," he said; "but I think that my old housekeeper will see to that now that I've put her on her mettle."

"I hope she'll prove worth the trouble you are taking and that her appearance will make as good an impression upon you as her voice seems to have made."

Forge grinned. "We shan't have long to wait; they may be here at any minute."

When the visitor did arrive they had to own that, however attractive her voice was, it could not have been more prepossessing than her appearance. She had even succeeded in dispelling the habitual gloom of Huskisson, who introduced her first to her host.

The girl's manner was charming. "But how kind of you to ask me here," she said to Forge, looking at him from beneath her long lashes. She was tall and slender with a kind of ethereal beauty about her which seemed to Forge very unlike the usual type of Frenchwoman. It would have been difficult to describe the exact colour of her eyes, which seemed to change from grey to green. Oborn made an inward note of their extreme intelligence.

Forge, intent on hospitality, demanded whether she had dined and, learning that she had not, ordered a tray to be brought. He knew that he could leave to his housekeeper the choice of the viands.

Pauline Coulon allowed a dinner wagon to be wheeled in and helped herself to the various good things without showing the least concern because three pairs of eyes were fixed upon her; moreover, she plied a good knife and fork while chattering away about her impressions of the first Christmas she had ever passed in England.

"Your Christmas," she said, "I know is the *fête* for children but at Waterloo one sees little of that; everyone seems to be hurrying homeward as fast as they can and most of them are laden with parcels."

It was Huskisson who first introduced the subject that was uppermost in all their minds, although they had avoided it until now.

"Mademoiselle Coulon was, of course, very much upset at the news I had to break to her."

"Ah yes!" She threw out her hands with a little gesture of horror. "But surely Margaret had no enemies in England. You have, of course, very clever police at your Scotland Yard. They are working on the case—yes?"

"Oh yes; their best men are working on the case," said Forge. "I should not be surprised if they called to see you as soon as they hear that you are in England and that you knew Margaret Gask well."

"But I know of no enemies that she had."

"Perhaps it was no enemy," suggested Oborn; "it may have been a friend."

"Friends do not kill defenceless women." Then she added thoughtfully: "But a jealous lover might."

"He might," said Oborn with meaning.

"You are forgetting the fur coat," said Forge, to whom this innuendo was distasteful.

"Fur coat?" she asked. "What has a fur coat to do with it?"

"Merely that it disappeared on the night of the murder."

"She was wearing it, you mean?"

"We think she must have been, as it was such a cold night."

"Then the motive was robbery?"

"The whole mystery is why was Margaret in the lane at that time of night," said Forge. "There could have been nothing to take her out except to meet someone."

"But what contradiction," she said with a little moue. "If she had a rendezvous it must have been with a lover and yet a lover, even if he killed in jealous rage, would not steal a coat."

"That's what puzzles us all," said Oborn. "I think perhaps if you had been here all the time your woman's intuition might have gone a long way towards solving the mystery."

"I don't know," she said. "Of course Margaret was very beautiful and a beautiful woman never lacks lovers." She passed her hand over her forehead and turned to Mr Forge. "You will forgive me but I have been travelling for so many hours and this news has upset me..."

"You would like to go to your room," said her host. "My housekeeper will show you the way and see that you have everything you require."

"Thank you: that will be very nice."

Chapter Seven

Dallas' next report, received after Boxing Day, read as follows:

> "In connection with what has come to be known as the 'murder in Crooked Lane' I have to attach the medical report of Dr Smithers on the death of Hyam Fredman. It will be remembered that at the inquest held yesterday the jury returned a verdict of 'murder by some person or persons unknown.'"

Richardson turned to the medical report and noted that it was in the handwriting of Dr Smithers himself. He touched his bell; a clerk answered it.

"Ah! You're the very man for this job," said Richardson. "You can decipher the handwriting of doctors who ought to be dropped into a canal with a stone round their necks as a warning to the profession to write legibly."

The clerk looked at the document with knitted brow. "Very good, sir," he said with resignation; "you shall have a typed copy but this is worse to decipher than most of them."

"I've often wondered," said Richardson, "how many deaths have been caused by chemists making up poisonous prescriptions because they can't read them. There must be an unholy pact between chemists and doctors to keep their dreadful secrets from the outside world on whom they both live. Let me have a transcript as soon as you can."

When the clerk had left Richardson turned again to Dallas' report.

> "We have established beyond doubt that Hyam Fredman was a receiver of stolen goods with a connection among persons who had access either as guests or serv-

ants to houses known to contain valuable property. He was suspected, though proof was never obtained, of receiving a masterpiece of an old Italian painter stolen by burglars from the house of Mr Eidelston, in Shepherd's Market, Mayfair, and disposing of it to a well-known receiver in Paris. In view of the fact that he was a receiver the following persons may be regarded at this stage of the enquiry as suspects:

"(1) The butler, Alfred Curtis, office number C.R.O.2753. To steal a valuable while employed as a servant on a forged character would be quite in accordance with his criminal record, though it is right to say that he has never been convicted of any crime of violence.

"(2) Arthur Graves. When we interviewed this man he said that his relations with Hyam Fredman were confined to borrowing money from him. A search of the money-lending books, very carefully kept by Fredman, do not disclose the name of Graves as a debtor but in a locked desk in the antique shop was found a receipt for £50 signed by him. This would suggest that he was disposing of stolen property. He knew both Hyam Fredman and Margaret Gask.

"(3) Gerald Howard Huskisson. This young man was known to have had a violent quarrel with Margaret Gask during which he or she was trying to wrest some solid object from the other's hand. This object could have been the emerald, stolen by one of the two. His statement that he retired to bed at 11 P.M. that night can neither be verified nor disproved.

"It may reasonably be assumed that Hyam Fredman went to Crooked Lane on the night of the nineteenth and received the emerald from Margaret Gask, who was either alone or perhaps accompanied by Huskisson. The finding of a revolver discharged in two chambers beside Fredman's body seemed to suggest that this pistol may have been used in the murder of both.

"The disappearance of the fur coat which Margaret Gask must have been wearing might support a theory that her murder was committed by an outsider simply for the object of stealing a coat that would have high value among furriers.

"Although there is nothing definite to connect Douglas Oborn with the crime there is a discrepancy between his statement that he did not know the murdered woman and that of the woman herself, who spoke to Mr Forge of looking forward to meeting Oborn as an old friend.

"Let me now return to the question of the revolver. The weapon lying by the body of Fredman is a Colt of an ancient pattern, rusty and ungreased. The three undischarged chambers contained cartridges and bullets that would fit the rifling. One of these cartridges has been submitted to a gunsmith who reports that the powder has been in the cartridge for a considerable time, probably not less than two years, since the grains showed traces of damp; indeed he was surprised to hear that the fulminate was still efficient in view of the evidence of damp. I authorised him to test one of the live cartridges in order to ascertain its penetrative efficiency: he found that the explosive quality of the fulminate was entirely destroyed and deduced that this must have been the case also with the two empty cartridge cases; moreover, neither of these two empty cases showed any sign of blackening. From these facts I submit that the weapon lying by the body of Hyam Fredman was placed there as a blind. We have traced the sale of this weapon. Mr Cohen, a pawnbroker in Sun Street, Kingston, has identified it as one sold by him to Hyam Fredman, who produced the necessary pistol certificate. Fredman told him that he wanted it as a curiosity, as he had quite a collection of ancient weapons. Against this is the fact that we found no other weapons on the premises of Mr Fredman: probably he wanted the revolver merely to intimidate possible burglars.

"The medical evidence disproves the idea of suicide. We have as yet no indication pointing to any person having visited the shop that night. As already reported, we had to gain access to the shop by employing a locksmith; we found the back door, leading into the yard, also locked but the key was missing. This would lend support to a theory that Fredman himself opened the shop door to admit the murderer, locking it behind him, and that the murderer made his escape through the back door, locking it behind him and taking the key with him and scaling the wall of the yard which would have given him access to a narrow lane. This theory is supported by scratches found by us on the surface of the wall, which is only eight feet high. The murderer may have hoped to induce a belief that Fredman had killed Margaret Gask and then committed suicide with the same weapon.

"In the case of Margaret Gask no bullet was found, which is not surprising, but in a later search of Fredman's room a flattened bullet was found which corresponded to an indentation in the brick wall at a height of five feet four and three quarter inches from the floor: this must have been the bullet which traversed Fredman's head.

"At this stage of the enquiry I did not think it wise to interview any of the persons who were staying at Scudamore Hall, for fear of alarming them. Mr Forge consulted me confidentially about engaging a private detective as one of his servants and I undertook to find him a man who could be thoroughly relied upon. Accordingly I engaged a retired detective inspector who undertakes private enquiries—ex-inspector William Spofforth—who is in the house now as an under butler. He fully understands the need for circumspection and he is not personally known to Alfred Curtis. I shall receive from him reports at two-day intervals. Mr Forge has promised solemnly that he will not divulge either to any of his guests or his servants the identity of ex-inspector Spofforth.

"In the meantime there has been an addition to the party at Scudamore Hall—a young French lady who had been an intimate friend of Margaret Gask. Though Mr Forge did not altogether approve I took an opportunity of interviewing this young lady in order to find out what she knew about the dead woman. At first she was reluctant to discuss her but at a second interview she was more forthcoming and gave me the following information: six months ago this lady, Mlle Coulon, entered the service of the Henri dressmaking firm in the Rue Royale, Paris, as a mannequin. The star mannequin in this establishment was, she said, Margaret Gask. On pressing her for further particulars she told me in confidence that Margaret Gask appeared at big social functions beautifully dressed by Henri with jewellery on loan from Messrs Fournier, Rue de la Paix; that she was wearing at a ball at the Opera House a valuable diamond clip which she 'lost.' On this she was discharged. I begged Mlle Coulon to tell me in confidence whether there had been any doubt about the loss being genuine and she admitted rather evasively that this had been the case. I asked her whether she had kept in touch with Margaret Gask after her dismissal from the firm and she admitted that she had. It was about that time that Margaret met Mr Forge; Mr Huskisson was also in Paris.

"All this goes to confirm our belief that Margaret Gask was a woman who lived on her wits and was probably concerned with others in thefts. One point that we have not yet cleared up is how she came into contact with Hyam Fredman. This point we are now working upon.

"ALBERT DALLAS, *Detective Inspector*."

Richardson had scarcely finished his perusal when his clerk returned with a typed copy of Dr Smithers' report.

"You've been very quick. I suppose long practice of deciphering difficult handwritings has made you an expert."

The clerk smiled. "I had very useful help, sir. Detective Sergeant Lomax was working in this department during the last days of the war and told me that he had had to decipher far worse scripts than this. Four words puzzled even him and we were going to leave them blank but in the end the context supplied the missing words."

"Thank you," said Richardson; "that is all for the moment." He picked up the typed copy of the report and read as follows:

"I have this day made an examination of the body of Hyam Fredman. He appeared to be a man of a little over forty, well nourished and inclined to corpulence. All the organs were healthy. The cause of death was a bullet wound which had traversed the brain from left to right. The man must have been standing at the time, for the orifices of entry and exit were placed horizontally. I made a search for this bullet: it was not there. There was, however, on the brick wall a mark as if a bullet had flattened itself against the brickwork: the flattened bullet must have been carried off by the murderer. The weapon found within reach of the murdered man's hand could not, in my opinion, have been the one used by the murderer: the orifice of entry was too small to have been made by a bullet of the calibre of the Colt revolver found on the floor near the body.

"J. SMITHERS."

Richardson took the report in his hand and went with it to the door of one of the luminaries of the legal department, which had lately been taken over by the commissioner's office at New Scotland Yard. He was a keen-looking solicitor of about forty with a long experience of preparing briefs for the Criminal Bar. Richardson had acquired the habit of consulting him on the general principle that two heads are better than one.

"Look here, Mr Jackson, would you run your eye over this last report of Dallas' and the medical report attached; both bear upon that murder case in Crooked Lane."

"What I should like to know," said Jackson when he had finished reading the report, "is what valuables this man Forge keeps in his house. He seems to have a little gang of suspects about him: they can't all have been after a single emerald, however valuable."

"Dallas put that question to him and was invited to look over the house. He says that it was handsomely furnished in a modern way and that there were a number of silver ornaments of no great value but the plate was not solid silver."

"Is he a collector of pictures, china or anything like that?"

"I believe not."

"What's your opinion as to why these people have collected at Scudamore Hall for Christmas?"

"In my opinion they belong to the sort of gang that is glad to batten upon any rich man and get the run of their teeth during what is commonly described as the festive season."

"Well, I can't give you any theory regarding the identity of the murderer without getting a good deal more information about the people than appears in Dallas' reports but my own feeling is that the motive for both murders was not robbery, but revenge or fear."

Chapter Eight

AT FIVE O'CLOCK on the second day after Christmas Mr Forge entered his house and made for the drawing room, as being the place where he was most likely to find his guests assembled. He found only one—Mlle Coulon seated at a well-furnished tea table. He paused on the threshold to admire the very attractive picture that she made.

"See how I am being spoiled," she cried gaily. "Your butler insisted that I must have tea at five o'clock. He said that all ladies in England drank tea at five and that you would never forgive me if I did not conform to the custom of the country. I reassured him. I told him that in Paris it had been the custom, too, for many years. So here I am with the teapot ready before me and only lacking congenial company. That you have come in time to supply. Do you like your tea weak or strong?"

"Strong, please," said Forge, taking the vacant chair opposite to her. "I suppose that the other men are out, though they are not tea drinkers."

"Your butler told me that you were all out; that is why I did not wait."

"I'm afraid that you are having a very dull time, mademoiselle."

"Oh, not at all. I have always longed to see English life: it is so little understood in France."

"I'm afraid you are not seeing an English Christmas at its best. I had arranged for a house party with all the old Christmas merrymaking but then came this sad business of poor Margaret..."

"I am so sorry for you, monsieur. This tragedy must have upset all your plans. No doubt you had arranged to welcome your relations..."

"I have none, or at any rate relations so distant that I do not know them. No, I was looking forward to a Christmas party of friends. The fact is after wandering about and staying in foreign hotels and rooms in London I began to think that it was time for me to settle down and that is why I built this house."

"It's a charming house on the edge of this lovely moor and now your plans are all being spoiled. I understand." She nodded sympathetically.

"Sometimes I toyed with the idea of marrying. I'm very lonely."

"I see," she said again and added softly, "To Margaret perhaps."

"Well, I must confess that the idea had crossed my mind." He sighed; the ready sympathy of this attractive girl and the intimacy of the tea table seemed to warm him into confidences.

"I am not surprised; lots of men fell in love with Margaret."

"Tell me about her."

"Well, there is not much to tell. When I first met her she was the star mannequin at Monsieur Henri's establishment. We others were almost jealous of her because it was she who wore the newest creations and the jewels and I can assure you that when dressed for a show she was a dream."

"When I first met her in my hotel in Paris she was not employed anywhere."

"And so she became your guide and interpreter, yes?"

"Well, in a sense, yes. You knew her well. Tell me why she quarrelled with Monsieur Henri?"

"Oh, they had a difference of opinion about the clothes she was to wear and she was very high spirited and left him."

"Did you know many of Margaret's friends?"

"Some of them, yes."

"Did she ever speak of a Mr Oborn?"

"Never. Why do you ask?"

"Well, when she heard that he was one of my invited guests she said that he was an old friend and that she would be pleased to meet him again and yet Oborn himself declares that he never met her."

"That is strange. Of course I didn't meet all Margaret's friends. Mr Huskisson knew her well and spent a lot of time in Paris this autumn. Have you asked him to explain this little mystery?"

"Yes, and he says, like you, that he never heard Margaret speak of Mr Oborn."

At this moment the person they were speaking of made his appearance.

"Ah!" he said gaily. "This is where you are. Huskisson is looking for you, mademoiselle. He says that he promised to give you a lesson in billiards."

She jumped up. "Ah! I had quite forgotten I promised to be in the billiard room at half-past five."

When the door was shut behind her Oborn remarked, "Perhaps this is a budding romance. Huskisson seems very much taken with her."

Forge took him up rather indignantly. "What do you mean? Huskisson was in love with poor Margaret; he could not have forgotten her in four days."

Oborn shrugged his shoulders. "Of course I never had the opportunity of seeing the two together, but he seems quite to regard Mademoiselle Coulon as his particular property."

"Well, that's quite natural. He knows her better than we do and they were friends in Paris."

"Is Mademoiselle in a position to clear up the mystery of Miss Gask's friend, my namesake?"

"It's funny you should ask me that. I had just been questioning her on that very subject. She had never heard Margaret mention anyone of your name."

"Ah well!" responded Oborn; "then that little mystery goes to the grave with her."

"The mystery of her death also seems equally unlikely to be solved. Would you like to know my own opinion? It's this. We all know that she had many admirers. I think that some jealous blighter followed her over from Paris, made this rendezvous with her at midnight, shot her and bolted back over the Channel by the very next boat."

"My view is less romantic than yours. I think that some blackguard killed her for the sake of her coat and perhaps jewels—if she was wearing any."

"But that does not explain why she was in Crooked Lane at midnight. She must have gone there of her own free will."

"True; your idea of a rendezvous must be correct but a lover would never steal her fur coat."

"Well, we'll have to leave it to the police to unravel the mystery. After all, it isn't our job."

Meanwhile the lesson was proceeding in the billiard room but there were gaps in it for conversation.

"Ah!" exclaimed Pauline after missing an easy shot. "I shall never have time to learn this difficult game before I go back. You see in France our billiard tables have no pockets."

"But the pockets are a help to the beginner."

"Yes, but I have to go back so soon there will be no time to practise…"

"Why must you go back? I know that our host wants you to stay and no business engagements are made at Christmas time."

"You forget that our great *fête* is New Year's Day and I must be back for that."

"Pauline, are you still employed by the Henri establishment?"

"Yes, I'm not yet among the unemployed."

He spent a few seconds in chalking his billiards cue and then went on, "Tell me, Pauline: you know as well as I do, don't you, that Margaret left Monsieur Henri under a cloud?"

"Yes, I know."

"Do you know why the matter was hushed up?"

"For many reasons. Publicity of that kind does no good to a firm. Also, Monsieur Henri, like most men, had a soft corner in his heart for Margaret."

"But who paid the jeweller's firm for the loss?"

"Monsieur Henri had to stand that but you must remember, my friend, that according to Margaret's story the jewel was *lost* in the Opera House. No one could prove that the loss wasn't genuine. It was never recovered, although the police had the matter in hand."

"Then if it wasn't proved there was no sufficient reason for dismissing Margaret. You must not think that I wish to blacken her memory now that she is dead but I think that Monsieur Henri had a stronger reason. Was it not in connection with the sale of his new models to American buyers?" She was silent and he went on, "Believe me, I am not asking out of idle curiosity."

"In that case, and knowing that you were Margaret's friend, I can say that your guess is correct."

"And the fur coat which is now missing, did that not belong to Revillon?"

"That, my friend, cannot be proved, as the coat is missing. If it were recovered…"

"But it is true that a valuable mink coat has been lost by Revillon and Margaret was never employed by that firm."

"That coat had been bought by Henri and mysteriously disappeared from his workroom: all the workers are beyond reproach."

She put her finger on her lips because at this moment the new under butler, Spofforth, opened the door noiselessly and brought in a coal scuttle for making up the fire. As soon as he had retired Huskisson returned once more to the subject of Margaret Gask.

"Tell me one thing while we are alone: had Monsieur Henri any suspicion against Margaret over that jewel?"

"Do you know what the jewel was?"

"A diamond brooch, I believe."

"It was—a very valuable one—with a special safety device that could not be released except by someone who knew the secret. Monsieur Henri and the jeweller had themselves fitted it into Margaret's corsage."

"I see," said Huskisson gravely.

Pauline looked at him while his face was averted; there was a look of conjecture in her expression.

"I can see what you are thinking," she said. "You believe that Margaret may have succumbed to the temptation to possess herself of Mr Forge's emerald: he told me about it."

Before he had time to answer she darted noiselessly to the door and flung it open. This brought her face to face with the under butler: clearly he had been eavesdropping but he was in no wise disconcerted. He smiled at her deferentially and said, "I have just come to give Mademoiselle a message from Mr Forge; it was to know if you would care for a game of bridge before dinner."

She looked at the clock on the mantelpiece. "I'm afraid there's barely time." She turned to Huskisson with a smile. "Mr Forge has not yet learned how long it takes a lady to dress for dinner. If I'm not to be late I must go to my room now. Our host looks like a man who would hate to be kept waiting."

She was about to enter her own room when she looked back and saw that Spofforth had stopped to set his watch by the clock on the landing. With a mischievous smile she turned from the door of her own room and dashed across the landing to the room that Margaret Gask had occupied. She switched on the light, shut the door behind her and after opening wide the wardrobe stood there waiting for the knock that she felt sure would come. It came almost instantly. She opened the door and gave a realistic start on seeing Spofforth.

"Pardon me, mademoiselle," he said politely, "but Mr Forge has given directions that this room is not to be entered."

"I did not know. All I wanted was to see the room my poor dead friend occupied but I will leave it and not enter it again without Monsieur Forge's permission. You are a new servant, are you not?"

"All the servants in this house are new, mademoiselle," he responded, moving aside for her to pass out.

She left with a quite natural air of meekness.

Chapter Nine

Report from Detective Inspector Dallas, December 28:

"The Assistant Commissioner, C.I.D.

"Sir,

"In continuation of my report of the 26th inst. I have to add the following. Discreet enquiries regarding the movements of Arthur Graves have disclosed that he made frequent visits to Paris; on his return from each of these visits he changed his address in England, putting up at country hotels in the southern counties more often than in London. In view of facts that have come to light during the course of our enquiries I think it essential that a French-speaking officer like myself should go over to Paris to make further enquiries about Arthur Graves and certain persons now staying at Scudamore Hall. Speed is essential in order to circumvent attempts from the guilty person or persons to defeat the course of justice and therefore I am asking your permission to cross to Paris tomorrow evening.

"I attach hereto a report from ex-inspector Spofforth, who is now acting as under butler at Scudamore Hall.

"Albert Dallas, *Detective Inspector.*"

Richardson turned over the sheet with a feeling of curiosity. He had known Spofforth when he was a third-class sergeant in the C.I.D. and he was curious to see how he would comport himself as a private detective in what promised to be a complicated case. The report ran as follows:

"SIR,

"In accordance with your instructions I had an interview with Mr Forge at Scudamore Hall on Christmas Day and presented your letter of introduction. He appeared to be greatly relieved by my coming and promised to assist me in every way that lay in his power; evidently he has been greatly upset by the recent events in his house. I impressed upon him that no hint of my identity should be allowed to reach the other servants and he kept his word, for I found that the servants assume my engagement to be due to Mr Forge's expectation of having numerous other guests during the festive season. As the house has only recently been opened and the servants are all newly engaged there was no suspicion attaching to me of being other than I represented myself to be. It is needless to say that I am keeping a watchful eye on the butler, Alfred Curtis, who has a long criminal record. I find this man very civil and considerate to those working under him; there is nothing about him to suggest that he has a criminal record. The only suspicious circumstance that has come under my notice was that this morning I interrupted what appeared to be a confidential conversation between one of the guests, Mr Oborn, and Curtis. I should not have thought this worth including in my report if I had not noticed that the interruption caused by my entrance appeared to discompose Mr Oborn.

"Among the servants the murder of Miss Gask is a constant subject of conversation but apparently none of them knows anything about the theft of the emerald. The general opinion among them is that Mr Forge should have contrived to get rid of Mr Huskisson, who is regarded by them with deep suspicion based on the fact that he and the dead woman were known to have had a violent quarrel and he was the last person seen with her that night.

"I am not yet in a position to report anything definite about Mr Huskisson, who is by nature a gloomy young man who is indisposed to respond to any kind of greeting when one passes him in the hall or corridors; he appears to have much on his mind but this is not to say that he is hiding some guilty knowledge. He seems to be on very friendly terms with the young French lady who had been invited to Scudamore Hall by the dead woman. I have overheard them discussing the subject of Miss Gask's death and her mode of life in Paris. I have a suspicion, but only a suspicion, that if Miss Gask stole the emerald it was with the knowledge, if not the active collusion, of Mr Huskisson.

"The behaviour of Mlle Coulon, the young French lady from Paris, is not in my opinion above suspicion. She seems to want to search the dead woman's wardrobe, for the maid who waits on the ladies told me that she had found the door of the wardrobe ajar and is certain that the clothes belonging to Miss Gask had been disarranged from the positions in which she put them; apparently someone had been making a hasty search among them. Yesterday when I was keeping observation from the end of the corridor I saw Mlle Coulon cross from her own room to that occupied by the dead woman. She was there but a moment before I knocked at the door and opened it. I found the wardrobe open. I explained to her that Mr Forge had given orders that no one should enter the room. She apologised and crossed to the corridor to her own room. I have gathered in conversation that the dead woman, Mlle Coulon and Mr Huskisson were all friends together in Paris.

"With regard to Mr Oborn, the other member of the house party, Mr Forge seems convinced in his own mind that he was acquainted with Miss Gask, although he disclaimed any previous knowledge of her. As Miss Gask is dead it is impossible for me to clear up this question, because the evidence available would be entirely on one side. I have had a conversation with the constable at Kingston who preferred the charge of dangerous driving against Oborn. Although at the hearing Oborn produced evidence that appeared to be incontrovertible, this constable is convinced that his witnesses did not invent their evidence about the number of the car. He is so positive that I cannot believe him to be entirely mistaken and I propose to devote some time and trouble to get at the truth of these conflicting statements. I have persuaded the authorities of the A.A. to assist me in clearing up this discrepancy.

"WILLIAM SPOFFORTH, *ex-Detective Inspector.*"

Richardson marked the paper "further report" and laid it on one side to await the arrival of Detective Inspector Dallas, who was coming to ask for permission to go to France. He had not long to wait; the familiar rap sounded on the door and Dallas presented himself.

"Good morning," said Richardson. "I have been reading this report of ex-inspector Spofforth, the man you engaged for Mr Forge. He seems to be a careful sort of man."

"Yes sir, he is very discreet and careful. If he has a fault it is that he starts by suspecting everyone he meets and letting each of them dispel his suspicions if he can."

"Well, that's not altogether a bad way to work provided that it is fairly done."

"Yes sir, and in this case, in which there is no actual suspect, there is much to be said for it."

Richardson nodded. "My practice is to put an officer in charge of a case, give him a free hand and ample time and leave him to clear it up. Now, about this trip of yours to Paris. Is it really necessary? Could not we find out what you want to know by writing to the Sûreté?"

"I'm afraid not, sir. We have of course already got from them some information about Miss Gask but I am of opinion that by interviewing her last employer I might get information that would form the basis for further enquiries in this country. As you know, I am anxious to trace the connection between Hyam Fredman and Miss Gask and so far I have not succeeded in getting any evidence on this. We have strong reason for believing that the dead woman met Hyam Fredman in Crooked Lane and passed the stolen emerald to him. In further searching Fredman's shop we came across this." He took from an inner pocket of his tunic an official envelope and unwrapped from its tissue paper a clip of platinum from which all the stones had been removed.

Richardson turned over the empty platinum setting curiously. "I think I read in one of your reports that Miss Gask had been discharged by her employer for having 'lost' a diamond clip of great value."

"Yes sir, and I want to show this to Monsieur Henri and see whether he recognises it. From Miss Gask's passport I have gathered that she has not visited England until this time for eight months but that jewel was lost only six months ago, so she must have an accomplice."

"Always supposing that she stole the jewel and that her story of having lost it was untrue. Yes, I suppose that it is the only course to take. The Receiver will kick at the cost, so you must keep your expenses as low as possible and not be too long away."

"I don't think that the Receiver will raise any difficulties, sir."

"Why not?"

"Well, sir, I think that Sir William rather likes the idea of the reputation of this department standing high on the Continent. You will remember that in the case of those drug traffickers, the case that the newspapers called the murder in the barn, our co-operation with the French police produced excellent results and notably raised our reputation in Paris."

"Well then, you'd better go ahead. I hope that you will find Monsieur Henri willing to co-operate with you." Dallas smiled a little self-consciously. "In the past I have been fairly successful in obtaining the good offices of any Frenchman I've had to work with."

"Ah! Because you speak French."

"No sir. I make a point of never speaking French when I'm in Paris, because then the French talk among themselves in the belief that I do not understand what they are saying and I look stupid and drink in every word. It is a great help."

"Do you mean you have an interpreter?"

"Not with a man of the type of Monsieur Henri, who speaks a halting kind of English, but the police authorities always provide me with a man who speaks English."

"Very well, go your own way to work as long as you're satisfied that it's the best. Have you any suspicion against any of Margaret Gask's friends that we know?"

"So far no very definite suspicion but either Huskisson or Graves could have been in league with her."

"Do you mean that either of those men fired the shot that killed her?"

"I don't rule out the possibility in either case, sir. Mr Vernon and I are quite agreed from enquiries and observation kept on Arthur Graves that he is a shady character; we have established the fact that he made frequent visits to Paris."

"I have discussed this case with Mr Jackson, of our legal department, and I think that I may tell you the theory that he formed."

"I should like very much to hear it, sir."

"It was only a very general opinion, namely, that robbery was not the motive for the two murders, but revenge or fear."

"That squares very much with my own theory, sir. I'm glad to have it supported by the opinion of a man so competent and clearheaded as Mr Jackson. Mr Vernon's idea is that both murders were connected with the possession of the emerald, but though the stone no doubt has a high intrinsic value it has no history and its value would scarcely be sufficient to account for two murders."

"Have you ever asked Mr Forge how the jewel came into his possession?"

"Yes sir; it was a quite unromantic story. It was in the hands of a French marquis who had been speculating heavily on the turf and he had to dispose of it in a hurry to meet his obligations. His name has escaped me for the moment but I have it in my notebook."

"Well, I should advise you to tell the story to one of your French colleagues and see whether he can give you any useful information regarding this French nobleman who had it."

"I will, sir."

Richardson again took up the report and said, "I see that your man Spofforth appears to be suspicious about the young Frenchwoman who has turned up at Scudamore Hall. Do you agree with him?"

Dallas smiled. "The lady in question doesn't strike me as being in the least likely to be a criminal or to be associating with criminals, but I must admit that there was an element of drama about her arrival at Scudamore Hall. She told me that she had been invited there by the dead woman, Miss Gask; that she telephoned from Waterloo to Mr Forge, not knowing that Miss Gask was dead and that he very hospitably invited her to come. All this has been verified by Mr Forge, but in answer to my questions he admitted that Miss Gask had never mentioned having sent the young lady an invitation."

"Well, I suppose you will include her in the list of people you will enquire about in Paris. In the meantime we can do nothing. You had better get your momentous interview with the Receiver over. If he makes difficulties come to me again."

Chapter Ten

MR FORGE had been opening his morning letters at the breakfast table. He looked up unhappily.

"Another batch of refusals this morning. It is disheartening to find how a death in the house casts a shadow over it. Though they don't say so one can read into all these refusals the same cause—the fear of passing the holiday season in a house where there has been a sudden death."

"Perhaps it is because people regard the holiday as over and done with," suggested Oborn.

"But the people I asked don't belong to the class which has to work for its living. And I had so hoped to make things a little livelier for Mademoiselle."

"You are very kind, but I am one of the workers and my holiday leave will be up tomorrow," said Pauline.

"What! You are going to leave us so soon?"

"Alas! but I must. Remember, I work for a dressmaking firm and our *fête* in France is the New Year. People want new clothes for the *fête*."

"I also have a job to attend to," said Huskisson. "They want me to take a consignment of cars over to Paris."

Forge looked up sharply. "I doubt very much whether you will be allowed to leave the country."

"Who'll stop me?"

"Why, the police. As I understand it, they don't want anyone to leave this house until that case is cleared up."

"But how can they stop me?"

"It's the simplest thing in the world," broke in Oborn; "they have their fellows at the ports and aerodromes: all they have to do is to put your name on the gate and withhold a permit to embark either by sea or air. They do this every day."

"Hell!" muttered Huskisson under his breath. "It's a free country and I shall go whatever they say."

"Try it and I think you'll find that the country is not as free as you like to think it."

"But it would be monstrous to stop you going abroad on legitimate business. Even in France that is not done," said Pauline. "I shall expect to see you in Paris next week."

"You will," said Huskisson firmly.

Forge looked profoundly uncomfortable. He did not get on very well with either of his male guests. Of the two he preferred Huskisson, but he had an uneasy feeling that this guest had become an object of suspicion to the police and he did not at all look forward to a brace of constables ringing his bell and marching one of his guests off between them. It would be a climax to the local reputation of Scudamore Hall. Of course all the servants would leave in a body...

"I shall put this confounded place in the hands of an agent to let or sell," he muttered.

Pauline cast upon her host the kind of indulgent glance that she would have assumed towards a pettish schoolboy. "You, monsieur, must come over to Paris and enjoy its gaiety; then you will forget all these worries and return later on to this charming house feeling that it is to be a home for you. Time, as you say in England, is the great healer."

"I should not mind so much if you were not going, mademoiselle. Is your decision irrevocable? Can we do nothing to dissuade you?"

"Alas, monsieur! You must not try to tempt me. I thank you for a delightful holiday and if you will invite me again at some future time I shall accept your invitation with enthusiasm."

The rest of the day passed uneventfully. There was more than one argument between the men as to which of them should have the agreeable task of seeing Mlle Pauline off by train, but Huskisson won the day and drove her up to Waterloo in one of Mr Forge's cars. It must be confessed that, unknown to Pauline, they tossed for the privilege.

Armed with a platform ticket, Huskisson escorted her to her compartment. It was already occupied by three people and on such occasions the occupants are all ears for the partings of travellers who are to be their stable companions as far as the port: it made conversation constrained. When the porter had slammed the doors of the compartments Pauline put her head out of the window. "Good-bye. I shall see you in Paris next week," she said.

Huskisson almost hissed through his clenched teeth, "Yes, if these damned police don't stop me from crossing the Channel, but I'm afraid they will."

"Your police seem to think that when they find that fur coat they will also have found the murderer. I think they are mistaken."

He could not ask her why, as the train had begun to move. Pauline settled herself, took from her handbag a notebook and began to read it critically, interpolating a few words here and there.

She had taken the day train, which arrived in Paris about 6 P.M. She put her suitcase into a taxi and directed the chauffeur to drive her to the address of M. Henri in the Rue Royale. On arrival she found the doors closed, but she rang the bell, which was answered by a liveried porter.

"Good evening, Jacques," she said. "I'm back again as you see. Is Monsieur Henri still here?"

"Yes, mademoiselle, and he is expecting you. We will leave your suitcase here and I will take you up in the lift."

M. Henri was a typical specimen of the prosperous French businessman—stout, florid and growing bald. He received Pauline with cordiality.

"Ah! You have come at a good moment. You have brought news? Yes?"

"Yes, but not as definite as we wished. I'll tell you all my discoveries and you can judge for yourself. To begin with, I obtained an invitation to the house by pretending that I had not heard of Margaret's death. Mr Forge was kindness itself. When he heard that I had come over from France expressly to stay with Margaret at his house he insisted that I should come."

"You did not tell him your mission?"

"No, monsieur; that would have been fatal to my success. He knows merely that I am employed here as a mannequin and that I was a friend of poor Margaret, but he does *not* know that I am a private enquiry agent recommended by the Sûreté to enquire into the thefts that have been committed in your workroom and showroom."

"Did you trace that fur coat?"

"I convinced myself that Margaret Gask had that fur coat, but it was stolen on the night she was murdered. I got an excellent description of the coat from the maid who waited on her and I am positive that it was our coat. I discovered also in her wardrobe at least two models that had belonged to us and I found this."

She produced from her handbag a label with the words "Henri. Paris." He examined it.

"This may very well have been taken from our coat. It is stouter than the labels that we put in dresses. I wonder how the British police failed to find this when they searched the room."

"I, too, monsieur, but we must remember that to a man like a British police officer a label of this kind would mean nothing; to us, of course, it means everything. So far I have avoided making communications to the British police and I want to discuss with you whether I should now take them into my confidence."

M. Henri pursed his lips doubtfully. "Are they intelligent, these British police—or are they heavy witted?"

"Well, I have not met many of them. Even now there is one in Scudamore Hall whose mission was to watch me—as well as others. He is masquerading as under butler and his waiting at table leaves much to be desired. One is lucky not to receive a shower of green peas down the back of one's neck when he is handing round the vegetables. He mounted guard at the end of the bedroom corridor and it was very obvious that he was watching me."

"Such a man would not find our coat."

"No, monsieur, and I doubt whether he could distinguish mink from rabbit fur."

"Monsieur Verneuil, of the 8th Arrondissement, has been here once more. He is a man of quick intelligence, though his training as a naval rating and his appearance give one the impression of heaviness. He has again examined the premises and he showed me how impossible it would be for a thief to enter without leaving a trace. He has again questioned Jacques, the night porter, and is satisfied that he was telling the truth when he declares that no one could enter at night unknown to him: even if he closed his eyes for a moment both doors are heavily barred inside. Then what remains? This is Verneuil's theory. He thinks that the actual theft was committed some days before we at first thought possible; that the coat was taken by Margaret Gask herself."

"But she had been gone some time."

"You were away for a fortnight. Margaret Gask was discharged, but a few days later she came back to ask my permission to take certain garments that were her property: she may then have had the opportunity that she looked for of taking the coat in the suitcase."

"But how simple if that's the explanation. It does not say much for the supervision in the workroom."

"Well, you were away and so was Madame Pernot, the supervisor."

"The idea is feasible. This is the first time I hear of Margaret Gask's visit to fetch her clothes. Certainly the mannequins' dressing room is next to the workroom."

"Monsieur Verneuil has established as a fact that when Margaret Gask called for her clothes she went to the workroom to bid the girls good-bye at the moment when they were leaving for lunch. It would have been possible for her at that moment to abstract the coat. Ah, that woman—what she has cost me! A coat worth thirty thousand francs and jewels worth a hundred thousand, for I had to make good that diamond clip. But, tell me, did you find no trace at all of that coat? I think you must communicate with Scotland Yard: they have a great reputation."

"You remember when we read in the English paper that Margaret Gask had been murdered and that a fur coat belonging to her had disappeared mysteriously, we decided that I should go over and try to discover whether it was our coat. This, I submit, I have done and Monsieur Verneuil's theory confirms it. The question is: Shall we get the Sûreté to move Scotland Yard, or would you prefer that I get into touch with that organization myself?"

"I think we will ask the advice of Monsieur Verneuil." He picked up his desk telephone and called a number.

"Is that you, Monsieur Verneuil—yes, yes. Put me through to him, please." When the connection had been made Pauline watched him with an indulgent eye as he danced from one foot to the other in his Gallic excitement. Suddenly he stiffened and his eyes goggled. "You say that he is here? But what an opportunity! He is now in your room? Yes, yes; I will be there in less than five minutes and I will bring with me Mademoiselle Coulon, fresh from England."

He put down the receiver and turned to Pauline. "Mademoiselle, an inspector from Scotland Yard is at this moment in Monsieur Verneuil's room. Let us both go and meet him there."

Chapter Eleven

RICHARDSON WAS READING a report that had just come in from Paris. He took up his blue pencil in readiness to mark certain passages, before sending it on to the C.I.D. Registry to have the former papers attached. It was signed "A. Dallas, *Detective Inspector*."

"In accordance with your instructions I crossed to Dieppe by the night boat and arrived in Paris at 6 A.M. I took a room in the Hotel Terminus and after breakfast I went round the hotels which were on the list supplied to me in order to ascertain whether Arthur Graves had registered in them and, if possible, to trace his movements during his visits to Paris.

"I was fortunate in finding the manager of the Hotel de l'Univers quite ready to tell me all he knew. He said that until about six months ago Arthur Graves had been in the habit of staying in his hotel four times a year. He was good enough to turn up the hotel register and show me his name. On the last occasion when Graves stayed there unpleasantness arose over a cheque which he had given in return for cash and the bank had dishonoured. Graves was voluble in his explanations and a French friend who had been in the habit of meeting Graves at the hotel came forward to cover the cheque which had been dishonoured, owing, he said, to a foolish mistake on the part of the bank cashier. The manager gave me the name of this French friend and his address, which he had given in consequence of questions about the dishonoured cheque. The address proved to be that of a small jeweller who executed repairs to watches and jewellery. I made the excuse of asking whether he had a second-hand watch for sale which he could guarantee as a good time-keeper. At first he shook his head, but on learning that I was an Englishman, as he had already gathered from my accent, he brought forward an expensive watch which he said he would sell far below its actual value. When I heard the price I told him that it was far beyond my means and I quitted the shop.

"Having learned so much from the manager of the Hotel de l'Univers, I did not think it worth while to pursue enquiries at other hotels, but I called on M. Verneuil, whose name you had given me, at the police office attached to the Grand Palais. He proved to be absent, but he was expected back in his office at 5 P.M. I did not wish to call upon M. Henri until I had seen Inspector Verneuil, but I went to the Rue Royale to look at the premises. The establishment appeared to be very busy; several cars containing ladies drew up while I was walking up and down.

"I then went to the private residence of M. Goron, to whom I had your letter of introduction. I was fortunate enough to find him at home. One seeing your letter he gave me a very warm welcome. I explained the main object of my visit to Paris and he told me that it would be well for me to see M. Verneuil, because he had been making certain enquiries and he knew that M. Henri was especially concerned in keeping the whole matter as secret as possible, for fear that police enquiries might militate against his interests.

"M. Goron was greatly interested when I told him about the murders of Miss Gask and Fredman. He said that he was convinced in his own mind that Miss Gask had been a professional thief; he had come across traces of her in investigating cases of foreign buyers who paid high prices for stolen advance models. He had no doubt in his own mind that she was mixed up with a gang of very clever and unscrupulous people and he suggested as the motive for her murder either revenge for taking more than her share of the spoil or fear that she would betray the gang to the police if she was arrested.

"M. Goron reiterated his desire to help us in every possible way but explained that at the moment he was very much occupied with the murder case in the Boulevard des Invalides in which a senator had been the victim.

"At five o'clock I entered the police station attached to the Grand Palais and was told by the constable at the door that M. Verneuil had arrived and was upstairs. He received me cordially and listened attentively to what I told him. As he spoke no English I allowed him to know that I could speak French. When I mentioned the watchmaker, Bigaud, he became alert.

"'We have a dossier on that man,' he said. 'He is known to us as a receiver of stolen goods, especially objects of value from foreign countries—England, Germany, Switzerland and Italy.'

"I told him that Arthur Graves, who saw Bigaud on his frequent visits to Paris, was under suspicion by us though we had no proof against him and I asked him whether it would be possible to have observation kept on Bigaud's shop. He replied that this would be difficult unless we could undertake to inform the French police before Graves arrived in Paris. If we did that he would undertake to keep him under observation and enter Bigaud's shop as soon as Graves was seen to go in. It might even be possible to stop the transaction of selling property stolen in England. For this reason I suggest that it would be unwise to do anything that would debar Graves from re-entering France.

"I told M. Verneuil that my real object in coming to Paris was to get information about the friends and associates of Margaret Gask. I had already established the fact that Arthur Graves was one of them. I asked him whether he could arrange confidentially with M. Henri to give me a private interview at which perhaps one of his agents might be present. He said that this would be quite easy and while we were discussing the question the telephone bell rang. The message was from M. Henri himself, requesting an interview with M. Verneuil. It was arranged that if he would come at once to the Grand Palais he could see not only M. Verneuil but a detective from London.

"When M. Henri was announced I noted to my surprise that he was followed into the room by Mlle Pauline Coulon, to whom I referred in my last report as being one of the guests at Scudamore Hall. She was quick to notice my surprise. She smiled and said, 'I must explain my little deception, monsieur.' She went on to say that in reality she was a private enquiry agent in Paris; that she had for some time been employed by M. Henri to report upon the frequent thefts that had been perpetrated in his establishment. She had had occasion to suspect Margaret Gask but had been unable to bring any specific case against her for lack of proof.

"With the Frenchman's frankness in such matters M. Henri broke in here to say that Miss Gask was a very beautiful woman and he had for a time allowed his heart to rule his head.

"I said that I was employed in hunting down the assassin of Miss Gask and that I had come to Paris to ascertain who were her friends and associates. I then showed M. Henri the platinum setting of the clip from which all the stones had been prised out. He recognized it immediately by its shape as the ornament that Margaret Gask was supposed to have lost at the Opera. I told him that it had been found on the premises of a receiver of stolen goods in London. He became excited and asked me whether I had also found the missing fur coat that belonged to him. I said that part of my mission was to trace that coat but that up to the present I had been unsuccessful.

"Henri turned to the young lady and said, 'It was part of your mission to ascertain who were the friends of Margaret Gask. Can you not help M. Dallas?'

"She shook her head. 'I went out more than once with Margaret, but the only man friend she introduced to me was Mr Huskisson, whom she appeared to know very well indeed.'

"I asked her whether she could tell me if Mr Huskisson had been at the ball at the Opera House when the jewel was alleged to have been lost. She hesitated a little and then admitted that he was.

"M. Verneuil questioned me about Huskisson and I gave him full details about all the guests at Scudamore Hall as far as I knew them. He was surprised to hear that I had not taken him down to the police station to be interrogated. I explained that this was not permitted to the police in England but that he had been questioned at the coroner's court during the inquest.

"The interview dragged on for nearly two hours and it was not until the end that I obtained one piece of useful information from Henri, namely, the address of a furnished flat that he had taken for Miss Gask; she had lived there for a month.

"When M. Henri and Mlle Coulon had left M. Verneuil explained to me that two reasons had actuated M. Henri in keeping the matter from the police until now; first his affection for Miss Gask and second the harm that it might do to his business. I then told M. Verneuil how the emerald came into the possession of Mr Forge: that it had been an heirloom of the Marquis de Crémont, who had been compelled to dispose of it. M. Verneuil grinned: he seemed to know the story of this marquis very well. 'Ah!' he said. 'That gamin is always turning up in our work; happily for the moment he has been lodged in prison for obtaining money by false pretences and I hope that it will cool his heels. But I am very much interested in what you tell me, because if my memory serves we shall find in that marquis's dossier a mention of an emerald having been stolen from a jeweller in the Rue de la Paix; the emerald in question has never been recovered.'

"He took up his desk telephone and rang up some subordinate, telling him to bring the dossier of the *soi-*

disant Marquis de Crémont. When this was brought we examined it together; it contained a long list of the marquis's delinquencies with the dates. The emerald had been stolen from a jeweller's shop by a trick, but it had been impossible to prosecute him as the thief although he was strongly suspected, because the stone had never been recovered. The case for which he had been convicted and for which he is now in prison had been clearly brought home to him. His usual trick consisted in calling upon a jeweller and asking to see uncut stones. He would then take from his pocket a piece of thick paper on which was drawn a design for a ring. The paper had some adhesive material smeared on the back; he would lay it on the tray of stones brought for his inspection and in the course of voluble explanations take the paper up and remove from it one or more stones that had adhered to it. His method of disposing of his plunder was always the same. He would stay in a first-class hotel and make the acquaintance of some well-to-do Englishman or American and sell the jewel to him as a family heirloom at far below its real value. He is believed to have an English confederate, but so far we have been unable to identify him.

"We discussed the question of bringing Mr Forge over, together with other witnesses, and decided that, for the present, it would not be worth while to incur the expense. I think, however, it might be wise to let a discreet enquiry be made of Mr Forge whether an Englishman introduced the pseudo marquis to him or whether the marquis had an English friend staying at the same hotel. We shall probably find that the English confederate is identical with the man we are looking for. Pending your reply, I think that it would be wise for me to remain here and pursue my enquiries. Tomorrow morning I propose to question the concierge of the flat where Margaret Gask stayed for a month.

"ALBERT DALLAS, *Detective Inspector*."

Richardson took the report to Jackson of the legal department. He knocked and heard the voice of the man he wanted to see shouting to him to come in.

"I hope you're not busy, Mr Jackson; I've brought you a rather interesting report from Paris, bearing on the case of the Gask murder that we were discussing the other day."

"Let me have a look at it."

In moments of concentration Jackson converted his physiognomy into a network of criss-cross wrinkles. This and his baldness made him an unengaging object to the eye, but his unerring judgment and his grasp of an intricate case commanded the respect of all who had to deal with him.

Having read the report, he returned it to Richardson, saying, "My first guess was right: that woman was murdered because she knew too much. That ought to help you in finding her murderer."

"Do you agree with what Dallas says—that the confederate of this French marquis is in all probability the guilty man?"

"I won't go quite so far as that, but I do think that if you find that confederate you won't be far away from the man you want."

Chapter Twelve

FOR WANT of something better to do, Forge and his guest Oborn took their guns and went out on Marplesdon Moor to shoot rabbits. Huskisson had excused himself on the plea that he had business to transact in Kingston; he had gone by car.

When the two sportsmen returned Forge noticed that the Sunbeam was already back in the garage.

"Oh, I see Huskisson's back," he said to Oborn. "His business could not have taken him very long; he would have had time to come out with us."

"I'll bet that his business didn't turn out well."

"Why do you say that?"

"Only because I feel pretty sure that he wanted to find out whether the police would offer any objection to his leaving your hospitable roof and that the police know the proverb of 'A bird in the hand...'"

"If the police do hold him up don't you think that it's a bit thick? I mean, this is a free country."

"You never can tell how much the police know about people. I suppose that nine men out of ten in this country have something to hide..."

"Damn it! That's going a bit far. What should Huskisson have to hide?"

"Nothing that I know of, but remember that the police know about that quarrel Huskisson had with Miss Gask and he was upset by the coroner's questions at the inquest; that was quite enough to start suspicions about him."

"You're talking rot," said Forge shortly. "Well, you know your way about the place and I'll meet you at lunch." He turned into the library, shutting the door behind him.

He had not been there five minutes before the door opened to admit Huskisson, who said, "I hope I'm not interrupting you, but I want to see you alone."

"Come in; nobody's likely to interrupt us here. What's the trouble?"

"I don't want Oborn to know, but the fact is that I've been down to the police and they tell me that, as they put it, the gate has been put up against me leaving the country."

"Good Lord! Why?"

"They wouldn't tell me why, but one of them said that whenever Scotland Yard wishes to keep a particular man in the country it notifies the port officers and they refuse him leave to embark. It's the same if he tries to fly the Channel."

"Do they give any reason?"

"No, but I suppose that in their dunderheaded way they don't want any possible witness to leave the country until this rotten business about Margaret Gask's death has been cleared up."

"Don't think that I'm butting in on a question that doesn't concern me, but I attended that inquest and I couldn't help feeling that your attitude towards the coroner's questions would be quite enough to prejudice the police against you. You must remember that the professional policeman is bred up in an attitude of suspicion. Trust in his fellow creatures has so often been betrayed that he sits up and takes notice whenever anyone prefers to keep his private business to himself."

"The police are a cursed nuisance."

"Sometimes they are, I agree, but my experience is that it is always worth while to keep on the right side of them if one can."

During this conversation Huskisson was showing signs of growing irritation, but Forge took no notice of them. He was wound up and, like an alarm clock, he could not be silenced until the winding had run down. "Couldn't you slip round to the police station and tell the superintendent what that quarrel that you had with poor Margaret was about?"

"No, I couldn't. It is no business of the superintendent or, for the matter of that, anyone else."

"If I seem to you to be interfering in matters that don't concern me you must understand that the whole business is very unpleasant for me and I think that I have a right to be taken into confidence to a certain extent. Besides, I have some influence with the local magnates and I might be able to help." It was

Forge's weakness to imagine that some of the minor constellations of his part of the firmament revolved round him.

"I quite sympathise with your position," said Huskisson, losing his aggressive manner, "but if I told the police the subject of our quarrel it wouldn't help them. I'll tell you this much in confidence, that if I did tell the whole story it would be much to the discredit of Margaret."

Forge pricked up his ears. He belonged to that trying class of people who fasten like vultures on the reputations of their acquaintances. "You know something discreditable against Margaret Gask? I assure you that the secret will be quite safe with me."

"I'm sorry, but I can't tell you any more." He turned to the door and left the room abruptly.

Before Forge had had time to recover from his discomfiture there was a tap on the door, followed by the entry of Spofforth, the pseudo under butler.

"I'm glad to find you alone, sir. I thought that the other gentleman would never go."

"Why, what's the matter?"

"I've had a message from the police station ordering me to report myself at once to the head of the C.I.D. at Scotland Yard."

"Good Lord! What does that mean—that something important has happened?"

"I cannot tell you that, sir. I shall have to go and my going off suddenly may seem to confirm the butler's suspicion about me. It would ease the situation very much if you could invent some excuse for my absence today."

"What do you mean about the butler's suspicions?"

"Well, sir, he keeps dropping hints."

"What do you mean?"

"Well, sir, he says that it's a funny thing that another man has been engaged when everyone knows that the house is already over-staffed."

"But I told him that I was expecting quite a number of other visitors."

"I know, but he says that you had already a staff big enough to deal with a large party for Christmas. He's no fool, that butler—very wide awake he is."

"Well, I'll tell him that I'm sending you to London with one of the guns: something's gone wrong with its ejector and you're taking it direct to the shop where I bought it. Will that do?"

"Yes sir; I think that will do."

"Don't go and leave my gun in the train when you get to Waterloo or, worse still, in a bus."

Spofforth laughed. "That kind of mistake has never happened to me yet, sir."

Mr Forge prided himself on the diplomacy with which he had handled a difficult situation; he would have been startled if he had seen the note, addressed to Mr Oborn, which his butler brought in ceremoniously on a silver salver just after lunch.

> Look out for the under butler; I'm pretty sure that
> he's a tec in disguise.

An hour or two later Oborn sought out his host and found him in the billiard room disconsolately practising cannons.

"Ah! You've come for a game?"

"Well, no; I've come in the hope of finding you alone."

"Why, what's the matter? You look as if you've something terrible to report."

"In a sense I have. For some little time I've been uncomfortable about the attention that is being paid to the things in my room and, in order to make sure of my facts, I set an innocent little trap in the shape of a cotton thread which I gummed over the front of a drawer. This afternoon, on visiting it again, I found the cotton broken."

"Oh, there's not much in that. Probably the fellow that valets you was putting things away."

"But this was a drawer in which I kept my private papers and no servant would have any reason for going to it. After that affair of your emerald being stolen I thought that I ought to come and tell you."

Forge looked extremely uncomfortable. His complexion had deepened in hue. "Do you suspect one of my servants?"

"Well, to be quite frank I don't much like the looks of that under butler fellow who has only been here a day or two. I've caught him hanging about the place in a very suspicious manner."

"Oh! I can assure you that he's quite above suspicion. I have the very highest character for him."

Oborn touched his host on the shoulder. "He may be all you say, of course, but I think that you ought to know that I caught him sneaking out of Huskisson's room with a letter in his hand."

"Surely not?"

"Anyway, it leaves an uncomfortable feeling: that a manservant is rooting about among one's papers."

Forge's colour deepened and his eyes goggled. He took the plunge. "Well, my dear fellow, it will ease your mind to know that he has been specially taken on by me to solve the mystery of that theft. He is really one of the best detectives in the country."

"For one of the best detectives in the country, his manner of going to work strikes one as clumsy. Do you suppose that he expected to find stolen jewels in my drawer?"

Mr Forge looked shocked. "You must remember that these super-sleuths very often adopt a clumsy method as a cover for their subtle activities. It is far better to let them go their own way to work and this chap is engaged, not to watch my guests, of course, but to size up the servants. I shouldn't have mentioned why he is here if you hadn't come to me with this complaint. I hope you won't mention what I've told you to anyone else in the house, or you'll quite spoil his stroke."

Oborn laughed a little artificially. "Oh, you needn't worry. I shan't mention it to anyone. As far as I'm concerned he can go on with his little game."

Forge brooded over this conversation for the rest of the afternoon. He had an uncomfortable feeling that he had become a minnow among a lot of hungry pike and that he was no longer master in his own house. His brooding took the form of irritation against Spofforth and he decided to have matters out with him as soon as he returned from London. He left a message with the butler that the man should be sent to him as soon as he came in.

He was in his bedroom dressing for dinner when there was a knock on the door and Spofforth made his appearance.

"You wanted to see me, sir."

"Come in and shut the door. What did the gun people say?"

"That there's nothing wrong with the ejector except that it wanted a spot of oil; they lubricated it and showed me that it works quite well." He lowered his voice. "As for the visit that I really went to pay..."

Forge interrupted him impatiently. "Before you go any further let me tell you something. I don't know how you did it, but you've made my guests suspicious of you and in order to soothe him I had to tell one of them who you really are."

"I hope not; that would be fatal to any chance of success."

Forge wilted at the concern in the man's tone. He blustered in his own defence. "Well, what can you expect when you go blundering into their rooms and interfering with their papers?"

"Who says I interfered with their papers?"

"Mr Oborn." He repeated the story of the thread that Oborn had set as a trap. Spofforth was about to reply, but he checked himself in time and Forge continued, "Well, what about this visit of yours to the C.I.D. at the Yard?"

"They want a piece of information from you, sir, but they impressed upon me that you must give your word not to mention my journey or its object to anyone, however much they may badger you to tell them."

Forge became irritable. "What do you take me for—one of these street corner advertisers? Of course I shan't blab. What's the information they want?"

"They want to know if you can remember who introduced to you the French marquis who sold you that emerald."

"Of course I can remember: it was Mr Huskisson."

"Thank you, sir; that's all they wanted to know."

Chapter Thirteen

THE MESSENGER laid a bundle of papers on Richardson's table; with his usual quiet efficiency he contrived to bring all those bearing a green "pressing" label to the top.

"Anything special?" asked Richardson.

"Yes sir; a report from Inspector Dallas in Paris. I've placed it on the top of these papers."

Richardson laid aside his other work to make room for the report for which he had been waiting and read as follows:

> "Paris. December 31,
>
> "SIR,
>
> "The first thing that I have to report is that I have had an interview with the concierge at 7, Avenue Victor Emmanuel, where Margaret Gask had lived at the expense of M. Henri for a month in the early autumn. The woman was very voluble; she told me that M. Henri had author-

ised her to let the premises if she could find a tenant but that, owing to the depression, she had not succeeded in doing so. Would I like to look over the flat with a view to occupying it? I said that I would and she took me up to the first floor, which was rather crudely furnished in red velvet. It consisted of a large room looking out upon the courtyard, a bathroom and a bedroom at the back. There was access to this bedroom from the service stairs behind it. As M. Henri had had the flat searched very thoroughly I did not waste time by making another search. I told the concierge woman of Miss Gask's death and said that I was anxious to trace her friends so as to break the news to them. When she had recovered from the shock she ran into her own quarters and brought out five visiting cards which, she said, had been left by gentlemen who had called to see Miss Gask. She gave them to me to take away: they are attached to this report."

Richardson unfastened the cards and went through them, nodding his recognition of four of them but pondering over the fifth—that of James Oborn. This was a printed and not an engraved card and it had the address, Hotel de l'Univers, written in the corner. The other four cards were those of Huskisson, Graves, the Marquis de Crémont and M. Henri. He returned to the report.

"I asked the woman whether she could remember what these persons looked like. She shook her head. 'What will you, monsieur; all Englishmen are much alike—tall and elegant.' I asked her which of them made the most frequent visits and was told that with the exception of M. Henri they had made but one visit each.

"I went on to the Hotel de l'Univers and had an interview with my obliging acquaintance, the proprietor. I asked him whether a Mr Oborn had stayed in his hotel last September. He ran down the names in his guest book and showed me the name of James Oborn, who stayed for one night only. I asked him to see whether Arthur Graves had stayed there at the same time and found that he had. I then went on to see M. Verneuil at the police station attached to the Grand Palais and asked him whether an identity card had ever been taken out by James Oborn. To my surprise I found that he was in a position to give me the information immediately and even to produce the card with its photograph attached. He told me that the address furnished was that of an apartment house in the 9th Arrondissement. The photograph is not that of the Oborn who is staying at Scudamore Hall: it is that of an older and stouter man. I went to the address given and learned from the concierge that Oborn had stayed there for some time but had left at the end of November without leaving any address for forwarding letters. I asked for any letter that might have come for him. At first she demurred, but when I told her that I was working in conjunction with the police of the 8th Arrondissement she handed me one letter which, she said, had been received on the day following his departure. I gave her my name and the address of M. Verneuil and I took the letter back with me to his office. He gave me permission to open it and we steamed it open. I gave him a running translation of its contents and he allowed me to take a copy of the original. It ran as follows:

DEAR JIM,

I've had a rather serious tiff with Henri, who is not the lamb that he used to be. He has had a bad attack of indigestion over my story about the 'lost' jewel and it was all I could do to dissuade him from ringing up the flat-footed brigade and giving me in charge. The air of Paris is not agreeing with me at this moment and I am off to England. There is an old fool, an Englishman, staying in this hotel. He and I have got pally and he has invited me to go and stay with him at a place called Scudamore Hall. I am taking over some quite decent stuff for our friend Fredman, but I'll have to be careful about how I make contact with him. I don't want the flat foots to get across my track, in case they shoot off a line to their fellow nuisances in London. Those Yard people are the very devil!

Huskisson has also got an invitation to the old fool's hospitable roof, so I'm going to be strictly respectable until I feel safer. The address is:

Scudamore Hall,
   Marplesdon,
      Surrey,
         England.

For heaven's sake don't indulge your usual habit of using old letters as pipe lighters. If necessary I can get an invitation for you to the same haven of refuge.

Yours,

Margaret

"It is obviously essential that, if possible, the man who uses the name of Jim Oborn should be traced and that his relationship, if any, with Douglas Oborn should be established, but since he appears no longer to be in Paris and his whereabouts are unknown because he did not comply with the requirement to register his new destination with the police, he can probably be traced more easily by letters from the department to its opposite numbers abroad than by my endeavouring to trace him from Paris. In that case I will report myself to you as soon as I receive a letter of recall.

"ALBERT DALLAS, *Detective Inspector*."

Richardson rang the bell and sent for Superintendent Lawrence, the controller of the rank and file of the C.I.D.

"Have you sent off the report which Inspector Dallas was to have in Paris?"

"Not yet, sir, but it is all ready to go. As a matter of fact it ought to be on your table at this moment."

Richardson pushed over the pile of papers as yet unread and asked him to find it.

"Here we are, sir."

"I think that I may want you to add something. Hold on while I read it."

He read the report aloud.

"'Acting on your suggestion that we should endeavour to find out from Mr Forge who introduced the Marquis de Crémont to him, we sent for the private detective Spofforth and asked him to ascertain in discreet conversation this fact. His report has just reached us. Mr Forge told him that it was Mr Huskisson who made the introduction. The report also states that one of the guests, Mr Douglas Oborn, had penetrated his disguise and had accused Mr Forge of employing a detective to spy upon his guests. Mr Oborn told Mr Forge that he had employed a ruse to confirm his suspicion that his room was being searched and had fastened a slender thread to a drawer containing private papers in such a way that it could be opened only by breaking it and that he had found the thread broken. Spofforth declares that he did not go to the drawer and therefore could not have broken the thread if it was really fixed as alleged. Either someone else had been investigating and had broken the thread, or Oborn had invented the story in the hope of getting some admission from Mr Forge.'"

"Look here, Mr Lawrence," said Richardson; "you had better add a line or two before the letter goes off. I'll scribble out the paragraph that I want you to add." He wrote rapidly and then read it aloud. "'Before returning to England you should again get into touch with Monsieur Verneuil and see whether he can obtain for you an interview with the Marquis de Crémont, who, I understand, is now in prison. You ought to be able to get from him information about Huskisson or the mysterious James Oborn. When applying for this interview you should impress upon the French authorities that the interview should take place in an ordinary office with a fire and not in the visiting room usually provided, in which one has to face the prisoner behind two sets of wire netting with a warder between; moreover, even if one can make oneself heard above the din of other visitors the room is so cold that both the interviewer and the prisoner long to get the visit over.' There, Mr Lawrence, that ought to do for Dallas."

"Yes sir; I think that will do, but while I'm here I would like to consult you about this man Spofforth. If it is now general knowledge below stairs in Mr Forge's household that he is a detective in disguise it seems scarcely worth while to keep him there."

"But it was a guest who made the discovery."

"You haven't forgotten, sir, that the butler is an ex-convict and would have been the first to penetrate Spofforth's disguise?"

Richardson smiled. "No, I haven't forgotten that and I think that it may turn out to our advantage...We mustn't forget that he's employed by Mr Forge and not by us."

At that moment the messenger entered, carrying a visiting card.

"Who is it, Edwards?" asked Richardson impatiently.

"A Mr Forge, sir."

Richardson turned upon Lawrence with a smile and said, "You'd better stick here while I see him. Show him in," he added to the messenger. He was curious to see the man who had been so much in their thoughts during the last few days.

The messenger, who had tiptoed out, now returned, ushering in the visitor. "Mr Forge," he announced.

Forge was not in the least like the mental picture which Richardson had formed of him. Instead of the successful profiteer with "bounder" writ large upon him he encountered the deprecatory gaze of a trapped rabbit.

"Won't you sit down," said Richardson, pointing to the armchair reserved for visitors. "You wanted to see me?"

"Yes. I have come to you more for advice than anything else. In fact it is about that detective whom I took on as under butler on the advice of your man Dallas."

"Yes?"

"Well, it's this way. He's given himself away and I'm wondering whether he's the right man for the job, but I thought I'd better get advice from you before I sack him."

"I'm sorry. I could, of course, give you the name of another retired detective who takes private work, but in your place I should think twice before I changed. You see, if another man goes down to take over Spofforth's place, everyone will assume that he's another police spy."

"But why not send him off and do without any detective in the house?"

Richardson turned to Lawrence, who was standing at the end of the writing table. "Shall we tell him?" he asked.

"I think we might tell him after binding him to secrecy. Look here, Mr Forge; I must let you into a little secret in police work. When an effect has to be produced one adopts one or other of two opposing methods; either we make our enquiries secretly, or we make them as openly as possible, simply in order to produce an atmosphere of suspicion and alarm. We are now working this second method and from what you tell me it seems not unlikely to produce results."

Forge had wilted during these remarks and he now turned as if for protection to Richardson. "Does this gentleman mean that I'm to keep on this man Spofforth when everybody has tumbled to it that he's a detective?"

"Unless something happens in the meantime," said Richardson, "I suggest that you keep him on for a week and then if we have got no further you come to us again."

Chapter Fourteen

MR FORGE DESCENDED the stairs and the granite steps, which so many had trodden before him with apprehension, and crossed over to Huskisson's waiting car.

"Well," said that depressed-looking young man. "How did you get on? You don't look cheered by your visit."

"And I don't feel cheered. The little gang in that building are enough to depress anybody. When I asked them for advice as to whether I should keep on that fellow Spofforth they said, 'Why, man, you haven't given the poor devil time to pull his weight.'"

"They used those words?"

"Well, perhaps not those words exactly, but that was the impression they gave me."

"Well, it's always something that you got out of that building without being accused of shooting Margaret Gask. They've got in reserve on the other side of the street a row of cells and they used to have an unpleasant habit during the war of shoving people into them to cool their heels. There have been suicides in them, but of course when the inquest is called they put the whole of the blame onto the deceased."

"Are you pulling my leg?"

"Not a bit of it. There was a suspected spy during the war who hanged himself from the cell ventilator, so I've heard, and they just swept him up and planted him in Kensal Green, no questions asked."

"Look here, Huskisson, I'm in no mood for fooling. What I have to do is to make up my mind whether I'm going to keep on this detective under butler or sack him outright."

Huskisson dropped his bantering tone. "Which did they advise you to do in there? They must have said something."

"They did; they advised me to keep him on, at any rate for a week, and if nothing results from it to come and see them again. I tell you that an interview with this far-famed 'big five' takes away all one's appetite for lunch."

"If you really want my advice you will keep the man on. He's no fool, or they wouldn't have recommended him to you."

"But if that fellow Oborn spotted his disguise he must be a fool."

"Don't worry about Oborn," said Huskisson. "Probably he's only trying to get the wind up you, or he's playing to get you to dismiss this under butler of yours."

"Why should he do that? Have you got suspicions against Oborn?"

"We've all got our suspicions: this affair is getting on our nerves. Where's your friend Dallas?"

"Fooling about in Paris, I believe. I should have thought he could do more good over here than pottering round with the French police."

"Don't run away with the idea that the French police are a washout. They're a clever set of devils and if they're not quite up to our standard, remember that the law gives them a licence which is never allowed to our men."

"You mean that they can use what journalists call the third degree?"

"Not only that; they can use methods for getting the truth out of a man that our fellows would never dare to employ."

"Torture, do you mean?"

"Oh, dear me, no; that would be a good deal too crude for French policemen. It's true that in some police offices in Paris they use a little gentle persuasion to get a man to talk, but in the majority of cases the very sight of the persuasive implements loosens the tongue so that you can't stem the flood of confession."

"It must make police work very easy."

"It would if the confessions were true, but the French criminal is a person endowed with imagination and the police officers know it and make allowance accordingly."

"Well, all this is beside the point. What matters is that I'm going to keep on this fellow Spofforth for a week at any rate."

"That's obviously the thing to do."

They were approaching the gate that led to Scudamore Hall when they encountered a tall man in uniform on a motorcycle, who saluted them. Forge turned round to look at the cyclist and saw that he had dismounted and was turning round his machine.

"That was an A.A. scout," he said. "Apparently he wants to speak to us. Hadn't you better slow down and see what he wants?"

Huskisson brought the car to a stop. The big man on the motorcycle also pulled up beside the car.

"Excuse me, gentlemen, but are either of you Mr Forge?"

"That's my name," said Forge.

"Well, sir, can I have two or three minutes' private conversation with you on a matter of importance to yourself?"

Forge looked doubtfully at Huskisson, who said, "I'll take the car into the garage and leave you to walk up; it's no distance to the house."

As soon as Huskisson was out of earshot the big man said, "I want you to tell me something in confidence, Mr Forge. Is that car, the Austin Twelve, P.J.C.4291, still in your garage?"

"It may be out at the moment, but its owner is still staying with me and uses his car quite a lot. Why, what's the trouble?"

"You remember that the owner of that car was summoned for dangerous driving; that it was alleged that he had knocked down a woman and driven away without stopping. When the hearing came on he was able to prove that he was in another part of the country on the day of the accident."

"Yes, I was in court and heard all the proceedings."

"Well, sir, the A.A. have been making enquiries and they report that another Austin Twelve bearing the same registration number was taken over to France from Southampton a few days ago."

"How extraordinary! Has anybody told the police?"

"Not to my knowledge, sir. I think that the A.A. wish to get the case complete before notifying the police. That is why I have called to see whether the Austin Twelve bearing that number is still in your garage."

"Come up to the garage with me and you can see for yourself."

"Very good, sir. I may have to question the owner, but I don't want him to know that the other car with the same registration has been found."

"Right. I'll say nothing about it." He led the man up the drive straight to the garage, which was a large building containing three or four cars. "There, look round for yourself."

The A.A. man went straight to the Austin Twelve, took out his notebook, opened the bonnet and noted down the number of the engine and the other particulars by which cars are identified. He examined the licence affixed to the windshield and then asked to see Mr Oborn.

"Come along into the house," said Forge. "I think he must be at home, as his car isn't out. Do you want to see him alone?"

"No, I don't want him to think that there is anything secret about my enquiry. In fact I'd rather you were present."

As they were ascending the front steps Forge whispered, "I don't mind telling you in confidence that I have a private detective recommended by the Yard working as under butler here. If you'd like to see him before you go any further I can send him out to you."

"No, I don't think that at this stage that will be necessary."

Forge threw open the front door and rang an electric bell in the hall. The butler presented himself.

"Ask Mr Oborn to come to the library for a minute."

"Very good, sir." The butler's demeanour was unexceptionable. "I think he's in the billiard room."

Oborn was in the billiard room. Mr Forge would have been surprised if he had heard how the message was conveyed to him. The butler shut the door, looked carefully round and, lowering his voice to a lurid whisper, hissed, "There's a blinking A.A. scout asking for you. You'd better be jolly careful: he ain't nosing round for nothing."

"You let your suspicions run away with you. Where is he?"

"In the library, and take care is all I say."

Oborn was in no way disconcerted. He threw open the library door and wished the scout good morning. "What can I do for you?"

"It's this way, sir. The A.A. people up at Wakefield, who assisted you in that case in the police court, want to complete their logbook of assistance given to their members; they've asked me to have a look at your registration book for particulars."

"Righto! But I don't carry such things about with me. I'll have to go upstairs to get it."

"That's all right, sir; I'll wait here."

While Oborn was out of the room Forge smiled at the big man. "You did that very well," he said; "you must have had some sort of diplomatic training."

"No sir; but it's better not to meet trouble halfway. I meant to see that registration document and I didn't want the gentleman to dig his toes in and decline to produce it."

The door opened; Oborn handed the document to the scout, who examined it and said, "You've no objection to my jotting down the particulars, have you, sir?"

"None whatever."

"You ought to be jolly grateful to the A.A. people," said Forge. "I've always heard that they are friends in need."

Having taken the particulars he needed, the A.A. scout handed the document back to Oborn with a smile.

"Have you got all you wanted?" asked Oborn. If not, now's your chance."

"Yes sir, thank you. I've taken all the necessary particulars and now I've only to take my leave." He moved towards the door.

"Stop! You'll never be able to open that door unless you know the gadget," said Forge. "Let me do it for you: I designed the fastening myself. Now, just as an object lesson, see whether you can open it."

The scout gave a tug or two and grinned. "No sir; I fear that I must fall back on the inventor." He knew these amateur locksmiths and their chagrin at another's success in opening one of their special devices.

Forge pulled open the door. "There," he said, "it's as simple as A B C when you know how."

"It's a very ingenious device," said the scout.

Forge accompanied him down the steps. "I flatter myself that I did that rather well. I wanted to shake off that inquisitive gentleman so that I could ask you whether you found everything in order."

"Perfectly in order, sir. If there's anything crooked in the registration it isn't with this gentleman's car."

The reply was like a blow in the face for Forge, who was counting upon some sensational news to carry to the superior individuals at Scotland Yard.

"What are you going to do about that other car going about with a wrong number?"

"I'll have to report it to the headquarters and let them decide." The scout had his leg over the saddle of his motor bicycle as he spoke.

"But shall I not hear the result?" asked Forge in disappointed tones.

"Well, sir, I'll take care to let you know what transpires and meanwhile I'll ask you not to mention the case to anyone; most of our difficulties arise from people talking too much."

The noise of his engine drowned any protest that Forge may have made. The owner of Scudamore Hall felt that he was being slighted, but his passing annoyance was alleviated when he saw Spofforth carrying a bucket of water into the garage. Certainly the A.A. scout had enjoined silence upon him but that would never have been meant to apply to a detective recommended to him by the Yard itself. With a careful look round to make sure that they were alone he addressed Spofforth pompously.

"Some important evidence has come into my hands. I must not say how."

"Indeed, sir," replied Spofforth, humouring his weakness. "Perhaps I ought not to ask you the nature of this fresh evidence."

"I think it is in the interest of justice that you should know it."

"Does it bear upon the murder, sir?"

"Oh no, no; it's a different matter altogether." He told at great length the story of the A.A. scout's visit. He concluded by saying, "I don't believe that the man knows the proper course to pursue. I doubt if he will tell the police."

"Perhaps I ought to tell you, sir, that he is making his enquiries at the prompting of the police."

Mr Forge left the garage with the same appearance of deflation as a leaky balloon.

Chapter Fifteen

THE NEXT REPORT from Dallas was brought to Richardson at seven o'clock just before he was leaving the office for the night. It ran:

"In accordance with your instructions I saw M. Verneuil on the subject of an interview with the Marquis de Crémont. I cannot speak too highly of the co-operation of the French police. M. Verneuil used his telephone and my interview was arranged with the governor of the prison, who undertook to allow it to take place in a special room with armchairs and a warm fire. One of M. Verneuil's officers accompanied me to the prison and introduced me to the governor, who was obviously anxious to meet me in every way. He told me that the Marquis de Crémont was one of his most troublesome prisoners. 'In what way?' I asked him. 'Is he violent or disorderly?' 'No, worse than that,' he replied; 'he gives himself airs and never tires of demanding special privileges in accordance with his rank.' He said that this kind of prisoner was far more troublesome to the governor than the violent blackguard, because he was always scrupulously polite in his insistence and could not be dealt with for any breach of discipline. With this light upon his character I felt prepared to conduct the interview.

"The marquis proved to be one of those elegant, slim young men with perfect manners, a soft voice and a seductive way with him which would account for his success among women—particularly foreign ladies, who would be impressed by his manners and his long eyelashes. He would have had no difficulty, either, in impressing a person like Mr Forge. He approached the fire, rubbing his hands, explaining with a smile, 'The central heating at this hotel leaves much to be desired. I am going to make representations to its manager that if he wishes to attract guests he must really see to the heating.'

"I caught an exclamation of contempt from M. Verneuil's officer, who was in the room with us, but this in no way discountenanced the prisoner, who went on, 'I understand that you wish to see me, monsieur. I am always glad to be of service to gentlemen from the other side of the Channel: it fosters the *entente cordiale*.'

"With a man like this I adopted the sudden method of springing information upon him. 'You were acquainted, I think, with a lady named Margaret Gask. I have called to tell you that she is dead.' I expected some sign of perturbation from him, but I am sure I am not mistaken when I say that his expression was one of relief—the kind of relief that a criminal would feel when he heard of the death of a confederate who might round on him at some future time. His first impulse was to ask, 'Did she leave any papers?' but he tried to correct his slip by assuming an air of regret. 'I am very sorry to hear that, although I did not know her at all well.'

"'And yet,' I said, 'she counted you among her friends, together with others such as Mr Huskisson, Mr Graves, Mr Oborn and Mr Forge.' I watched his face as I mentioned these names and observed that he winced at the mention of each name. 'But they were all her fellow countrymen, whereas I was but a foreign acquaintance. I can't tell you anything about her.'

"'There is one thing that you can tell me about—that uncut emerald that you sold to Mr Forge,' I said.

"'Ah,' he sighed, 'that calls up sad memories; it was an heirloom in my family.'

"'You were introduced to Mr Forge by Mr Huskisson. Did Mr Huskisson suggest to you that Mr Forge would be a likely purchaser, or was it Miss Gask who suggested that?'

"He hesitated before replying and then he said, 'I think it was Miss Gask.'

"I asked him how he had come to know Mr Huskisson and he said that Miss Gask had introduced him. He could not, or perhaps would not, tell me anything more about his association with Huskisson, whom he represented as merely a casual acquaintance. When I asked him for his reason for getting Huskisson to introduce him to Mr Forge he said with apparent frankness that he had understood that Forge was a wealthy man and he himself was in pressing need of money and was therefore compelled to dispose of his heirlooms to the highest bidder. He denied all knowledge of either Oborn or Graves, but his denial was so emphatic that I felt sure he was lying.

"On my return to M. Verneuil I was handed a letter from M. Goron, asking me to go and see him on a matter which might prove to be important to both of us. Accordingly I went direct to his office and was at once admitted.

He quite overwhelmed me with his welcome. He said that he wished to place before me the facts of the murder case on which he was then engaged—the murder of the senator, M. Salmond. The following is a brief outline of what he told me.

"M. Salmond was a man of between fifty and sixty. He had taken a very prominent part in the recent disorders in the Chamber, always in the interests of the Right, who correspond roughly with our conservative party. Like other French public men, he had been deluged with abusive and threatening letters from his opponents, but he had never been assaulted in the Chamber or in the street and, as far as could be ascertained, had no private enemy. On November seventh he was found dead in the sitting room of his flat, which opened on to the main staircase: he had been shot through the head, the bullet striking him square in the forehead and traversing the brain. Search of the flat showed no sign of robbery; suicide was ruled out by the medical evidence and the police at first came to the conclusion that the assassin had been a person with some private grudge against him. With his will, however, there was a letter to his nephew, who was the principal heir. This letter stated that in the old Brittany cupboard in his sitting room a sum of five hundred thousand francs would be found between the newspaper lining and the shelf: he gave directions where the key would be found. On investigation this cupboard was found to be unlocked; it had been very cleverly forced: not a single franc note was found. This proved that the motive for the murder had been robbery.

"Without going into details M. Goron assured me that the persons who would have had access to the flat, including the deceased's nephew, had all been cleared of any suspicion. The notes were impossible to trace, as no numbers were known; they represented the hoardings of years. The flat had not been broken into; obviously the dead man had opened the door himself to the intruder. M. Goron produced for my inspection a number of voluminous reports from his staff to show me how thoroughly he had covered the ground. All tended to show that no stone had been left unturned in the question of the persons who could have known that the murdered man had this hoard of money concealed in his flat and where it was hidden: the result had led to no discovery. It was not positively known even to his relations that he had this money; it was merely conjecture among them, but it was a conjecture that squared with what they knew of his character. Some passing suspicion rested upon a certain Mme Fleuri who had for years been his intimate friend, but in the opinion of M. Goron she had been entirely cleared of suspicion. If she had been in want of money she could have had financial help from him to any extent without resorting to murder to obtain it. In a case of this kind the motive would not have been robbery, but jealousy of some other woman, and there was nothing to show that there was sufficient excuse for murder in any *affaire* in which the deceased had been concerned. In the course of M. Goron's investigations Mme Fleuri had admitted that for a time the murdered man had abandoned his habit of visiting her and this had occasioned a certain coolness in their relations, but he had since disarmed all suspicion that there was another woman in the case by resuming his former regularity.

"I suggested to M. Goron that the temporary break in the relations of these two persons might have been due to some other infatuation on the part of the man and asked him whether the result of his investigations supported this view. He replied that they had received information from a source not wholly trustworthy that M. Salmond had been seen dining with an attractive lady, who was a foreigner. The waiter who had volunteered this information was one of those people who were always ready to come forward with information if it seemed likely to please the person who was making the enquiry. M. Goron then came to the point which explained why he had sent for me. The wardrobe door which had been forced open had been wedged with a folded scrap of newspaper which had since proved to have been torn from the Paris edition of the *Daily Mail*. The fact that it was printed in English did not at first seem important, as all the drawers were lined with sheets from English newspapers and the concierge had explained that she obtained these newspapers from one of the flats upstairs, occupied at that time by English people; she preferred English newspapers because the ink did not set off and stain white linen as French newspapers do when used as linings to drawers. M. Goron had preserved the little scrap and on thinking the case over it had suddenly occurred to him that this wedge, if the issue of the newspaper could be identified, might afford a valuable clue. Accordingly his wife, who speaks and reads English, set herself the task. It gave no indication of date and therefore the undertaking was a formidable one. However, after some very painstaking work she was able to prove that it had been torn from the issue of the date of the murder. The newspapers lining the drawers were all three months older.

"M. Goron explained that he had now formed the theory that the waiter had spoken the truth: that M. Salmond had made the acquaintance of a beautiful Englishwoman and had taken her out to dinner, probably several times, and had betrayed, perhaps involuntarily, the secret of his private hoard.

"I asked him whether he thought that this woman had committed the murder; he said that it was more likely that the actual murderer had been a man but that she had furnished him with the information about the money and that he had used her name to gain admission to the flat. M. Goron went on to elaborate his theory, produced apparently from his inner consciousness and resting upon no evidence, that the murderer of M. Salmond and Miss Gask had been one and the same person. When I confessed that I could see no connection between the two he was surprised. 'It leaps to the eye,' he said. 'Surely you cannot have missed the point? Miss Gask betrayed the hiding place of Monsieur Salmond's money to a man; this man came to steal the money and shot Salmond; then because Miss Gask knew too much he followed her to England and killed her.'

"He then asked me about the people who were staying at Scudamore Hall on the night of the murder and we discussed the possible guilt of each one. He had a disconcerting way of ticking off each person on his fingers as if he were checking an inventory. Finally he said, 'Listen, my friend; my next task will be to ascertain in detail the movements of your Mr Huskisson when he was in Paris.' When I disclosed to him that Huskisson had introduced the Marquis de Crémont to Mr Forge in order to induce him to buy a stolen emerald he left his seat in his excitement. 'There, my friend,' he exclaimed as he walked rapidly up and down the room, 'there you have it. Crémont—a rascal—consorting with Huskisson, also a rascal and Miss Gask's closest friend. What more do you want?' At that moment the telephone bell rang and he was called away. In shaking hands he asked me to come in again the next day.

"A. DALLAS, *Detective Inspector.*"

Richardson laid down the report with a quiet smile flickering on his lips as he realised that Inspector Dallas had caught something of the dramatic fervour of his French colleagues in presenting his report, which was more picturesque than the usual formal report of a detective inspector. He rang the bell and sent a message to Superintendent Lawrence to come to him.

Chapter Sixteen

WHEN LAWRENCE presented himself Richardson put a simple question to him.

"Have you any further news of that Austin Twelve car that was taken over to France?"

"Yes sir; unfortunately our port officer in Dieppe did not get the order in time to stop the car, but he reports that the car left Dieppe with the avowed destination of the Riviera: this information was obtained in the ordinary way when an English car crosses the Channel. I was going to ask you whether we should get Inspector Dallas to drop what he is doing and follow up the movements of that car."

"No, you mustn't do that. Inspector Dallas cannot afford to spare a moment from his present case. We shall have to track that car in another way. Of course you've got the owner's name?"

"No sir; nothing was said about the name in the first telegram, but I wired for it and the reply is due at any moment."

"Well, let me have it as soon as it comes in. In the meantime, have you formed any opinion about the coincidence of the two car numbers being identical?"

"Well, sir, I should say that it was done deliberately, although we have verified the fact that Mr Oborn at Scudamore Hall did really register his car under that number."

"Well, couldn't Oborn be quite innocent in the matter? Couldn't the other man have taken the number without his knowledge?"

"Of course that's possible, sir, but it would mean forgery in the necessary papers and personally, I don't see how he could do it without Oborn's knowledge and help."

"It seems a very foolish thing to do unless the motive was overwhelmingly strong."

"Quite so, sir, but no doubt the motive was a very strong one—to hoodwink the police. Suppose, for instance, one or both of the cars had been employed in robbery or burglary."

"Well, one thing stands out: Oborn at Scudamore Hall must not be allowed to leave the country. You will see to putting up the gate against him at the ports."

"Very good, sir. That shall be done as it was in the case of Huskisson." He glanced at the clock. "That telegram should have arrived, sir. If you'll allow me I'll go and see where it is."

In three minutes he was back with an air of suppressed excitement about him. He had an open telegram in his hand. Richardson took it from him and read, "Name of owner of car James Oborn."

"So you see, sir, there are two Oborns."

"Yes, that bears out the evidence sent by Dallas from Paris that a James Oborn took out an identity card in that name. We must find out how these two men are related: brothers, probably. And yet Oborn said nothing about a brother when told by Mr Forge that Margaret Gask was expecting to see Jim Oborn."

Lawrence pursed his lips. "I think it would be a waste of time to question the man staying at Scudamore Hall: he would have a lie ready to suit his case. He appears to be a clever scoundrel and an educated man. Perhaps, sir, if you could arrange to get him down here and let us go through him we might succeed in tipping him off his perch."

"They might be able to trace the birth at Somerset House; you have his approximate age."

"Very good, sir; that shall be done and we won't send for Oborn until we've got our information."

"Owing to the accident in which that twelve-horse power Austin was involved in Kingston, we know that both James Oborn and Douglas Oborn were in England at the time of the murder of Miss Gask."

"And James has now escaped from our jurisdiction by going to France."

Richardson remained silent: he was thinking. "As we have Dallas on the spot in Paris," he said, "and this new information of the name of the man who has taken that car over seems to point to a connection with his present case, I think that he is the man for the enquiry. I'll dictate instructions for him while you are enquiring at Somerset House. As you go out you might send in young Williams. He's the quickest of your shorthand writers in Central."

"Very good, sir."

It was an hour later when Lawrence returned from Somerset House with the information about the brothers Oborn.

"I have been quite successful, sir," he said. "James and Douglas Oborn are brothers. The father was Walter Oborn, a solicitor in Salisbury; James is the elder son and was born two years before Douglas; there is a third son named Charles. I have telephoned to the Salisbury police, who tell me that the father died only three years ago; he never had a large practice, but he was above suspicion. Such practice as he had has been taken over by the third son, Charles, whose reputation is as unblemished as his father's. The Salisbury police have promised to make discreet enquiries about the other two brothers and will furnish us with a confidential report about them."

"You have ascertained that there is no criminal record against James Oborn?"

"Yes sir. Apparently they have never been detected in any illegality and that is why they still use their own name."

"You need do nothing more about Douglas Oborn. I will send him an invitation to call upon me: that will bring him unless I'm much mistaken in the gentleman."

"Very good, sir."

During the afternoon Richardson's messenger brought him a visiting card. "The gentleman is in the waiting room," he said.

Richardson glanced at the card and nodded.

"Show him in." The name on the card was Mr Douglas Oborn.

"Sit down, Mr Oborn. I've invited you to come down here in order to save our people a number of tiresome enquiries. I feel sure that you will do your best to help us."

If this opening to the conversation was disquieting to the visitor he did not show it. He sat down with an easy smile, saying, "Certainly; ask me as many questions as you like."

"Is your brother James in England at this moment?"

"Ah! That is one of the questions that I should find difficult to answer. I have not corresponded with him for some time, nor have I made it my business to keep in touch with him."

"When did you last hear of him?"

Oh, I should think it must be fully three years ago."

"And he was then...?"

"We met at my father's funeral at Salisbury and I remember that we lunched with another brother after the funeral."

"What is your profession, Mr Oborn?"

"Technically I suppose I might describe myself as a barrister of the Inner Temple; that is to say, I have been 'called.'"

"But you do not practise?"

His visitor laughed lightly. "No, I do not practise, because such solicitors as I know well have their own counsel, but if work were to come my way I should jump at it."

"You have chambers in the Temple?"

"Yes, in Fountain Court; you'll find my name painted up in number five and I have the honour of being allowed this privilege by the man who rents the chambers."

"I see; so you remain a practising barrister without any practice?"

"If you like to put it that way. I have on occasion done a little devilling for the man who gives me a seat in his chambers."

"That is the extent of your legal practice?"

"Yes, but you'll find my name in the law list if you care to look for it."

"You spend a good deal of your time abroad, I believe."

"Quite true. As you seem to take so much interest in my affairs, I may as well tell you that a few years ago I inherited a little money which has made me lazy."

"And your brother James—what is his profession?"

"You seem to be very much interested in the family, but, after all, we've nothing to hide. My brother James was to have entered the priesthood—my mother, as you may know, was a Roman Catholic. He found that he had no vocation for the calling and while he was making up his mind what he should do he, like myself, inherited enough money to make him lazy."

"And, like yourself, he spends a good deal of his time abroad?"

"He does."

"You have another point in common, I think. You both carry the same registration number on your respective cars."

"There you are better informed than I am. I know nothing about the registration of my brother's car: my own registration is perfectly in order."

"Well, it may interest you to know that your brother's car is in France at this moment and while we're waiting for it to return I must ask you not to move yours from Mr Forge's garage without notifying the police."

"I'm hoping to enjoy Mr Forge's hospitality for myself and my car for some days yet."

"When Mr Forge was so mystified at Miss Gask's reference to a 'Jim Oborn' why didn't you tell him that the Jim Oborn she knew was probably your brother?"

"I didn't think it mattered. My brother's friends are not necessarily my friends—especially his lady friends." There was a hint of disparagement towards the dead woman in his tone.

"Thank you, Mr Oborn. What you tell me is quite satisfactory and I need not detain you longer."

As the visitor opened the door into the passage he almost collided with Lawrence. He apologised, but Lawrence stood for a moment watching him before closing the door behind him.

"I see that you're interested in my visitor, Mr Lawrence," said Richardson.

"I am, sir. Was that Mr Douglas Oborn?"

"That was the name on his card; you see he accepted my invitation to an interview as I thought he would."

"Did you get anything useful out of him, sir?"

"He was so frank in his answers to my questions that I'm beginning to think that there must be something he was anxious to conceal. As we already know, his car registration papers are quite in order and we can do nothing more until we get hold of the brother, whose papers must be the forged ones: we shall then be in a position to judge whether the forgery was done with or without the knowledge of Douglas. I've sent the instructions to Dallas and told him that if he wants help you will send some-one over; it's obvious that he can't leave France just yet."

"No sir; that's quite obvious. If, as Monsieur Goron surmis-es, the murderer of Miss Gask also killed the French senator, he and Dallas working together may hit upon the solution at any moment."

"The murderer need not necessarily be Huskisson. Monsieur Goron seems very prone to jump to dramatic conclusions."

"I suppose you won't send for Huskisson yourself, sir, and put him through the hoop?"

"Not yet; that may come later. Have you received any report from Spofforth showing the impression that all these people have left upon him?"

"Not since the first one, sir; but he's been on to me by tele-phone this morning. He is suspicious of the butler. He may be prejudiced because the man is an ex-convict and therefore his suspicion of him doesn't carry much weight."

"What ground has he for suspecting him?"

"The chief ground is that he insists upon taking all letters from the postman with his own hand and on no account allows Spofforth, who as under butler might be given the task, to ar-range them on the slab in the hall."

"I suppose that Spofforth has noticed this because as a detec-tive he would like to look at the letters himself."

"Exactly, sir; and the butler is very clever in preventing Spofforth from examining the letters when they are on the slab. This is particularly awkward for us just now, when we are anx-ious to keep an eye upon Oborn's correspondence: any French postmark might prove useful. Spofforth also told me during our telephone conversation that Oborn and Huskisson seem to be suspicious of each other, and both of them carry their own let-ters to the post: there is a pillar box at the gate. Spofforth, see-ing them going out with letters in their hands, has offered more than once to take them to the box but has always been rather abruptly refused."

"Well, if those two men are beginning to suspect one another we honest detectives may come into our own."

Chapter Seventeen

TO THE LEAST acute observer the atmosphere at Scudamore Hall was becoming surcharged with suspicion and discomfort; more than ever was its proprietor disposed to seize upon an excuse for shutting the place up and becoming again a homeless wanderer in foreign hotels on the Continent. He was restrained by the knowledge that both his guests, Huskisson and Douglas Oborn, were debarred from leaving the country and the ban, he felt, was probably extended to him. It revolted him to think of the scene at the docks when a tall polite gentleman would be called up by the embarkation officer and after a whispered conversation would accost him and intimate that he would not be allowed to embark without authority from some mysterious powers in London. He knew too well that bluster would accomplish nothing; that threats to appeal to the home secretary or any other great power would courteously be waved aside, but that if he made any attempt upon the steamer's gangway a muscular arm would be put out to stop him with the intimation that he was blocking the gangway to the discomfort of the other passengers: he had seen all this happen to a vociferous person who, the rumour spread among the other passengers, was a noted criminal endeavouring to escape from justice. That was not the kind of ordeal that Walter Forge would care to undergo.

At this point in his reflections his ire rose against Spofforth. What the devil was the use of the man if he kicked his heels below stairs hunting for clues for days without finding out anything? Surely by this time he should either have cleared everyone of suspicion or have laid his hand upon the guilty person. In such crime romances as he had read the super-sleuth had only to gain access to the premises to lay his hand upon the shoulder of the culprit. Spofforth was not playing the game according to the rules. Besides, this Spofforth was producing tension between himself and his guests. Since they had discovered Spofforth's real vocation Oborn scarcely ever failed to refer to him humorously as the "tame sleuth", while Huskisson had withdrawn himself into a dense thicket of reserve.

That morning Huskisson had broken into open anger because Spofforth had taken a suit from his room, ostensibly for pressing and cleaning.

"But, my dear fellow," said Forge, "that is the ordinary duty of a valet."

"That might be all right if Spofforth was an ordinary valet, but we all know that he is not. The suit required neither pressing nor cleaning and, in my opinion, it was taken from my room for searching purposes. Probably the fellow went over it with a reading glass, looking for minute bloodstains."

Forge was shocked. "What a morbid idea. You must have been reading shockers from the railway bookstalls."

Huskisson left the room without another word and while Forge was plunged in gloomy reflection Spofforth broke in upon him.

"A gentleman has called to see Mr Douglas Oborn. I have his card here."

Forge took the card and read:

MR CHARLES OBORN
Solicitor
10, High Street, Salisbury

"This must be a relation. Have you shown him in?"

"The butler showed him in, sir, but he left this card on the table and I thought you might like to see it."

Forge, to whom nature had denied the more delicate instincts, rose and asked into which of the rooms he had been shown and on hearing that it was the library he bustled off there.

The greeting of the two brothers when Charles was shown in had been cold and formal on both sides. As soon as Douglas Oborn had mastered his surprise he said, "To what am I indebted for the honour of this visit?"

"I scarcely think that you need any explanation. I've come to ask a few plain questions and to get plain answers to them if that is possible to a person about whom the police are concerned. I can assure you that it is not very pleasant for a solicitor in practice in a gossipy little cathedral town like Salisbury to have detectives barging into his office with instructions from Scotland Yard to enquire into our family history."

"You said that you had come to ask questions, but so far you have been giving me nothing but interesting information."

"To begin with I want to know what you are doing in this house?"

"Oh, is that all. That question is soon answered. I was invited to stay here by the owner, Mr Forge."

"And Alfred Curtis? Why is he here?"

"He was already installed in the house when I came."

"Have you told your host that he was at one time employed by us as in indoor servant and discharged for dishonesty and afterwards convicted and sent to prison?"

"Oh, so you are one of those who, when a man is down and trying to make good, must come forward to ruin his chances. That is not my way."

"Can you truthfully say that you've had no dealings with Alfred Curtis during these past years?"

"Are you trying to insinuate that because you find him here as an indoor servant I must have been associated with him in dishonest practices?"

"God knows, no one could blame me for believing anything about you or James. You haven't forgotten, I suppose, that it was only by sacrificing half my capital that I kept you both out of the dock over that case of the Farnham trust money."

"And I hope you haven't forgotten that you inherited all our father's capital because you were the only one who hadn't been brought up in our mother's religion."

"Father had a stronger reason than religion for the precautions he took to ensure that the practice that he himself had inherited from his father should not suffer by getting into dishonest hands."

"Supposing that we leave our family history to take care of itself and you proceed with your questions. Let me see: I answered the question about Alfred Curtis. What is the next one?"

"Where is James?"

"I was going to ask you that very question myself. Where is James?"

"If you tell me that you don't know I must warn you that I shan't believe you."

At that moment Mr Forge's voice was heard outside.

"Ah!" said Douglas Oborn. "That is my host's voice. No doubt he is coming to be introduced to you and for once I shall really be pleased to see him."

Mr Forge made his appearance and put an end to further confidences between the brothers. He gave the new visitor a pressing invitation to lunch and it was accepted, because Charles was determined to have another private conversation with his brother before he left and also, if opportunity served, with the butler, Alfred Curtis.

Chance played into his hands because it transpired during lunch that Forge and Huskisson were leaving in the car for Kingston immediately after the meal.

"By the way," asked Forge, "how did you find the way down here?"

"That was quite simple. I came up by train to Waterloo and then changed into a Kingston train; from Kingston I took a taxi which nearly ruined me."

"Yes; Scudamore Hall is a bit remote and no doubt your taxi man took you the longest way round as they always do. Can we give you a lift back to Kingston?"

"Thank you very much, but my brother will drive me if I'm nice to him. I suppose you have your car here, Douglas?"

"Yes, and of course I'm anxious to see the most of you. Say the word and I'll drive you up to Waterloo."

"It will be the act of a good Samaritan."

"Well then, we'll be off," said Forge, putting out his hand. "Good-bye, and I hope that this won't be the last time you come down."

As soon as Forge's car had disappeared down the drive Douglas Oborn turned to his brother. "If you're ready I'll go round to the garage for the car. You mustn't think that I'm try-ing to speed a parting guest, but I have myself some business to do in Kingston."

"All right. I can defer my questions until we're in the car. I will start whenever you like."

Any surprise that Douglas Oborn might have felt at this ready acquiescence would have been dispelled had he seen his brother's next move. He rang the bell as soon as he was alone and when the butler answered it he drew him out of earshot of possible eavesdroppers.

"It's a long time since we last saw one another, Curtis," he said.

"It is, sir."

"I just want to say that I feel it my duty to tell your employer what I know about you."

"You always had a high sense of duty, sir; sometimes I used to feel that it might stand in your way. May I remind you, sir, of the saying that one good turn deserves another."

"I don't see how it applies in this case."

"In this way, sir. If your sense of duty compels you to speak to my employer, my sense of duty would compel me also to speak."

"What do you mean?"

"Your brother's conduct, sir, has not been quite above reproach and I think that you might find it embarrassing in your profession if it became known..."

"If what became known?"

"Certain strange stories, sir, about which you know nothing at present and it would be wiser for you to continue to know nothing."

The door flew open and Douglas Oborn stopped on the threshold. "Ah! I see that you're renewing old acquaintance."

The butler bowed and withdrew without another word.

"So you are in that rascal's power," said Charles. "You make a pretty pair—or trio, I should say, because no doubt James is in it up to the neck."

Douglas laughed sardonically. "So Curtis has been trying to make a bargain with you? If you tell of me I'll tell of them. Isn't that it?"

"Yes," growled his brother. "Let's get out of this quick. Where's your car?"

"At the door awaiting your pleasure."

Both men were silent during the first mile or so of the drive and then Charles adopted a conciliatory tone.

"Look here, Douglas; we can't wriggle out of the fact that we are brothers and both of us ought to think of the family name.

I happen to be a lawyer and if you've overstepped the mark in any direction I'm the man to advise you. You'd better lay all your cards on the table and make a clean breast of everything you've been doing."

"That's very nice and pretty, but I don't happen to have any sins to confess—at least nothing that it would do you any good to know."

"At any rate I feel sure you know where James is; you can at least tell me that."

"I'll tell you this much. James has been driving another car with my number on it and the silly fool has had an accident."

"I saw in the paper that you had been charged with dangerous driving and that you got out of it by proving an alibi."

"Exactly; the person who had the accident was James. He would have got out of it altogether if he hadn't been fool enough to take his car over to France with my number on it."

"Then he is in France at this moment."

"Yes."

"Do the police know this?"

"They do, but you as a lawyer know that dangerous driving is not scheduled among the offences for extradition."

"What on earth is the idea in having your cars labelled with the same number? It was bound to lead to trouble and to set the police wondering what the motive was."

"Oh, it won't do the police any harm to have to exercise what they call their brains, which are apt to rot with disuse. You see, I happen to be staying at a house that has come under police observation because a murder was committed there."

"All the more reason why you and James should play no foolhardy tricks."

"You can leave me and James to take care of ourselves; but for your peace of mind I'll tell you this. If James wants to hide in France he can get away from the cleverest sleuths in that country or this: no one could ever find him. By the way, you might have put your foot into it up to the knee if you had mentioned James to Mr Forge—but the Devil looks after his own. Although at one time he was dying to know all about a certain Jim Oborn, by great good luck he didn't connect you with him. And now we're getting into the thick of the traffic and you mustn't speak to the man at the wheel."

Chapter Eighteen

THE NEXT REPORT from Paris took Richardson by surprise: it had come by air mail and was marked "very pressing." The word "very" had been added in capitals to the ordinary "pressing" label.

"Having received from the landing officer at Dieppe a report that Arthur Graves had landed and had taken the train for Paris, I called upon M. Verneuil, who very kindly undertook to have a watch kept on the shop of the jeweller, Bigaud, and to have any Englishman who called there followed. The French detective seems to have been very astute, for at about three o'clock I received a telephone message to the effect that the Englishman Graves and the jeweller Bigaud had been detained for questioning and were at that moment at the police office attached to the Grand Palais if I desired to see them. I found Arthur Graves in a high state of irritation at his detention. He had been searched and on his person had been found a pearl necklace of considerable value. He was demanding to see the British consul. When he saw me he asked why he was being detained. I suggested that he should tell us how the pearl necklace came into his possession. After blustering for about five minutes and contradicting himself more than once he said that the necklace had been entrusted to him by the Marquis de Crémont to dispose of in England, but that, owing to the death of Fredman, with whom he had had transactions before, he had brought it back to France to see what Bigaud could do. He confessed that he had done business for the marquis on former occasions and that he understood that he was disposing of family heirlooms. But after close questioning by Verneuil, translated by me, and threats that unless he 'came clean' he might be held by the French police indefinitely, he became more reasonable and admitted that although he knew nothing he had guessed that the transactions were not above-board and that he would do well to walk warily. I pressed him for the name of any other confederate of the marquis. At first he disclaimed any such knowledge, but when I mentioned the name of James Oborn he said, 'If you know so much about these people why ask me? I'm only a messenger.'

"No further questioning or threats could get from him the whereabouts of James Oborn, and I am inclined to think that he knows no more than we do about this. He declared that though he had to meet him from time to time at the Hotel de l'Univers he knew nothing about his movements between these meetings and had never had any other address from him. The brother, Douglas Oborn, he had never met; neither had he met Gerald Huskisson. I then questioned him about Margaret Gask and after long prevarication I got from him finally that he had been entrusted by her with jewellery to dispose of to Fredman in England and that he suspected that these articles had not been honestly acquired. The rest of his statement about her tallied exactly with what he had told me at our first interview and I am inclined to believe that it was the truth and that he had not seen her on her last visit to England when she met her death. He could give me no information about any of her associates who might have had a motive for killing her.

"After a very long interrogation I arrived at the conclusion that this man was nothing more than a go-between; that he took to Fredman stolen articles that could not be disposed of safely in France and he took from Fredman to Bigaud things that could not be disposed of in England. For the moment the French police, whose powers are more extensive than ours, are keeping both Bigaud and Graves under preventive arrest. M. Verneuil has a strong suspicion that the pearl necklace is one reported by Mlle Saulnois, the actress, as having been stolen from her villa at Nice; steps are being taken to have an identification made.

"As soon as I received your instructions to trace, if possible, the car brought over by James Oborn I put the matter before M. Goron, who displayed an even greater anxiety to trace the car than I did. He circulated a detailed description of the car to the whole of his force of gendarmerie and promised to communicate any result of the enquiry to me. He seemed to think at first that he would be in a position to report results within a few hours, but so far I have heard nothing from him.

"Meanwhile he has been closely investigating the movements of Huskisson and up to date he has the following grounds for suspicion against him.

"(1) He was for some weeks the inseparable companion of Margaret Gask and was acting as her escort on the night when she 'lost' the diamond clip at the Opera House.

"(2) He introduced the Marquis de Crémont to Forge and knew that Forge had bought that emerald.

"(3) If, as seems probable, M. Salmond, the murdered senator, had had an affair with Margaret Gask, Huskisson would have been jealous and may have called on the senator from motives of jealousy and the robbery may have been a sudden impulse. On the other hand, if M. Salmond had communicated to Margaret Gask the whereabouts of his secret hoard she might well, in view of their relationship, have passed on the information to Huskisson and the robbery could have been premeditated.

"M. Goron is so convinced in his own mind of Huskisson's complicity that he is anxious to institute extradition proceedings for bringing him back to France to be charged with the murder of Salmond. I have pointed out to him that extradition would never be granted on such slender grounds.

"I have had another interview with Mlle Coulon. When I hinted to her M. Goron's desire for the extradition of Huskisson she laughed and said, 'You might as well apply for the extradition of Mr Forge, who is just as likely to be guilty.' Then she asked me if we had traced the fur coat and when I shook my head she said, 'And yet that coat is lying under your very noses—you British police.'

"I cannot help thinking that Mlle Coulon knows more about the disposal of the missing fur coat than she has yet admitted. I do not suggest that she is withholding information in order to impede the course of justice, but I think that there is at the back of her mind a desire to enhance the services of the French police and not allow Scotland Yard to carry off any of the credit should the case be solved. I hinted this to M. Verneuil, who nodded gravely but said that the young woman was very clever and could be entirely trusted to bring out the truth, giving credit where credit was due.

"ALBERT DALLAS, *Detective Inspector.*"

Richardson arrived at the signature with surprise, seeing that several other pages were attached. He began to read the next page with enhanced interest.

"I had just finished writing the foregoing report when further information of a most important nature reached me from M. Goron. He had traced the car and wished me to call upon him at once. On my arrival he lost no time in telling me that one of his men stationed in Montargis, about seventy miles from Paris on the route to the Riviera, had found the missing car in a garage in that town; that it had been brought in by an Englishman for repairs. On examining the engine the garage owner, Jean Robillot, had discovered that one of the pistons had seized, owing to defective lubrication, and that the repair would take two or three days. The Englishman seemed in a desperate hurry to go on; he said that he had to visit a sick friend and that it might be a matter of life and death. He suggested to Robillot that they should make an exchange—he taking a second-hand French car and leaving his own car in Robillot's hands. This exchange was effected.

"M. Goron suggested that he should drive me down in his fast car in order that we might investigate the transaction on the spot and this seemed to suit the interests of the department admirably, especially as there seemed to be no question of expense. Accordingly we started at once and reached Montargis in little over an hour. We found Robillot in some perturbation because he had had a visit from two members of the gendarmerie and he did not understand what the trouble was about; he had acted with perfect good faith and the Englishman had got a fair exchange. Was it suggested that the Englishman had sold him a stolen car or that he was discontented with his bargain? M. Goron soothed him tactfully and asked to be allowed to inspect the car. Robillot pointed out that the number plate appeared to have two numbers— one displayed on the front and the other on the back. He asked me whether this was the custom in England. I said that it was not usual and when I asked him what papers had been handed over with the car he said that the vendor had insisted on taking all the papers away on the plea that they would be useless to any new owner as they were English.

"M. Goron and I searched the car carefully but found not a scrap of any document beyond the licence pasted on the windshield. This had the same number as Douglas Oborn's car—P.J.C.4291. On the reverse side of the number plate was the number A.L.N.576. We removed the number plate and I shall bring it with me when I come; meanwhile perhaps you will be able to have enquiries made about the second number, A.L.N.576.

"A careful examination of the licence on the windshield betrayed the fact that the last figure in the date had been tampered with—1936 was made to appear as 1937. The licence may have been that used by the brother last year, cleverly altered to serve when necessary on this car. We obtained from M. Robillot a detailed description of the car which he had given in exchange for this Austin Twelve. It was a Citroën of 1931, in good condition and painted a light beige colour. Robillot protested volubly that his car was as good as the car he had taken in exchange, but when twitted by M. Goron he had to confess that in very wet weather she would stop suddenly, owing to water getting into the ignition; but as the purchaser was on his way to the Riviera he was not likely to encounter wet weather.

"I enclose herewith full details of the engine and construction of the Austin Twelve car in order that its history may be traced. If you require the car or the licence to be sent over please let me know as early as possible.

"M. Goron has now issued a circular order to his staff to trace the Citroën car now being driven by James Oborn. I should be glad to receive instructions by return as to what charge I am to hold him on.

"ALBERT DALLAS, *Detective Inspector.*"

Richardson laid down the report and rang the bell for Superintendent Lawrence, who had an engaging habit of collapsing on the carpet, or so it seemed from his attitude, when required to deliver counsel to a higher authority. Richardson had felt on many occasions what a loss he was to the light comedy stage.

"Now, Mr Lawrence, I have a conundrum for you, as my expert adviser upon French criminal procedure. Inspector Dallas is hot on the trail of James Oborn, against whom we have nothing but a charge of dangerous driving and using a false number on his car. These offences were committed in this country, but he is now outside our jurisdiction in France."

Lawrence's reaction to this address was, as Richardson had foreseen, to collapse on the carpet or to disintegrate into his component parts so that nothing could be done to clear up the mess except by using one of the patent vacuum cleaners.

"Well, sir, those are the only definite charges that we can make against him at the moment, but we have reason to suspect him of having been concerned in the murder of Miss Gask."

"H'm. We should have all our time cut out to prove a charge of that kind."

The component parts of Superintendent Lawrence were beginning to reintegrate. "Yes sir, we should, and when it came to getting the Bow Street magistrate to authorise extradition proceedings we should find ourselves up against it."

"There are occasions when the quality of legal proceedings has to be strained and this is one of them if we are to get any further in this case. Inspector Dallas has, in addition to his flair for detective work, a marked ability in coming to a friendly understanding with foreign officials."

"He has, sir; but I was thinking about Sir John Coulter at Bow Street."

"Well, we must get Dallas to persuade his friends in the Paris police force to hold Oborn for us until we've drawn the cord closer round him. Will you send him the necessary instructions?"

Chapter Nineteen

SPOFFORTH HAD SPENT an almost sleepless night, for he was now face to face with a sensation new to him: that of being himself a suspect. There was no reticence about his fellow servants below stairs; the butler had even attempted to draw him out upon the practice of the Yard in its attitude towards ex-convicts who were trying to make good. True, he had given him evasive replies, but he could not shake off the feeling that the butler was poisoning the minds of his fellow servants against him and that he was beginning to be looked upon by them as a spy. The fact that the house had been the scene of a murder was enough to upset the nerves of most of them and Spofforth realised that his position would soon become untenable.

The attitude of the people above stairs was no more reassuring. He had been engaged with a specific object, namely, to investigate the murder of Miss Gask and the theft of the emerald, and so far he had been unable to make any discovery of importance. Mr Forge, as he knew, regarded him as a hopeless failure; Mr Oborn treated him with open and contemptuous amusement.

It would require some dramatic development to restore his position, but whence could such development come? Of all the people he was called upon to watch, the man who seemed to have some secret to hide, if one might judge from his manner, was Gerald Huskisson, but so far there was nothing tangible to support this suspicion. He had made an exhaustive search in drawers and cupboards, outhouses and the grounds for the weapon that could have killed Margaret Gask, but with no result. Even a meticulous attention to the correspondence that came to the house produced nothing; in the rare opportunities that he had had for steaming open letters his labour had been lost, and both his employer and his guests had a habit of screwing up their letters and throwing them into the fire. There had been, it is true, one small discovery that afternoon. Huskisson had always shown a rooted objection to having his suits taken out of the room to be brushed. This in itself was sufficient to put Spofforth on his mettle. If there were nothing compromising in the pockets, why this objection to having the suit brushed downstairs as in every well-regulated household? That afternoon he had had the luck to find a suit belonging to Huskisson lying on a chair in his bedroom; he had taken it away and gone rapidly through the various pockets. In the watch pocket of the waistcoat he had found a cloakroom ticket for Waterloo Station dated December twentieth. He had quickly noted down the date and the number. On returning the suit to Huskisson's room, neatly folded, he had come upon its owner, who turned upon him furiously, demanding why his suit had been taken from the room.

"It was perfectly well known to Curtis that I objected to having my clothes brushed downstairs and he must have told you."

"No sir; doubtless he forgot to mention it."

"Then I'll give him hell for forgetting it."

Why all this heat? Had the suit anything to conceal? Could it be that that little cloakroom ticket hid the clue to an important secret? If so, Huskisson must be an exceptionally foolish person to have made a fuss about a trifle and so have drawn suspicion to it. Spofforth began to toy with the idea of what would happen if he took the particulars of that ticket to Waterloo and asked to be allowed to examine the contents of the package. Clearly the cloakroom attendant would refuse, quite properly, to allow the package to be searched unless he were accompanied by a senior officer of the C.I.D. Before he had finally dropped off into an uneasy sleep he had made up his mind to consult Chief Constable Richardson on the possibilities of getting a look at this package.

When he took in Mr Forge's early morning tea he asked permission to run up to town for a couple of hours.

"Where are you going?" asked Forge.

"To the Yard, sir."

"You don't mean to say that you have found out something?"

"Not exactly, sir; but I want to consult the people up there."

Forge had no consideration for the feelings of his subordinates. "Well, while you're up there you might ask them whether they think that you are doing any good by stopping here."

"I will, sir." Spofforth left the room hoping that his visit to the Yard would produce something that would restore his own self-esteem.

On arrival he was informed by the doorkeeper that Mr Richardson was engaged with Superintendent Lawrence and would not like to be disturbed, but he would send up his name and in the meantime he could take a seat in the waiting room. He was not long kept waiting. The messenger entered the room and enquired his name and on hearing it told him that both the chief constable and Superintendent Lawrence would like to see him at once. He followed the messenger into the chief constable's sanctum.

"I'm very glad to see you, Mr Spofforth. I want to hear how you are getting on."

"I thought you would like to know, sir, that Mr Douglas Oborn received a visit yesterday from his brother, Mr Charles Oborn, who is a practising solicitor in Salisbury."

"Ah! We knew, of course, about this brother. Were you able to glean anything about the object of this visit?"

"Not very much, sir; but I was able to gather that the two brothers, Charles and Douglas, were not on very friendly terms. Another fact which may be important is that the butler, Alfred Curtis, seems to have some kind of understanding with the Oborns. I know that Charles, the solicitor, had a private conversation with Curtis."

"In view of the fact that Curtis is an ex-convict this development is certainly important. You had, of course, no opportunity for gathering the gist of their conversation, but you must not relax your efforts to find out what the connection is between them."

"This is very difficult, sir, because it is now clear that Curtis suspects me, but I will do my best. Mr Forge was indiscreet enough to tell Mr Oborn that I am a detective and if I am right in thinking that he has an understanding with the butler he would have passed the information on to him."

Richardson forbore to point out that it was owing to his own clumsiness that the nature of his employment had been guessed by Oborn.

"To turn to another person," said Richardson. "What do you make of Huskisson? I understand that the French police entertain suspicions against him."

Spofforth brightened. "Then perhaps, sir," he said, "the little matter I have to see you about will not seem trivial." He went on to describe Huskisson's dislike of having his clothes removed for brushing and mentioned the finding of the cloakroom ticket in one of the pockets.

"A cloakroom ticket!" exclaimed Lawrence. "I once brought a murderer to justice with nothing more damning in the way of evidence than a cloakroom ticket. Did you take possession of the ticket?"

"No sir, because I did not wish to excite Mr Huskisson's suspicions, but I've taken full particulars of the ticket—the date and so forth. Here they are." He handed a slip of paper to Lawrence.

"December twentieth," said Lawrence. "Why, that is actually the day following the murder of Miss Gask."

"We shall have to examine this package in the cloakroom," said Richardson.

"Yes sir; but I could not hope to get the cloakroom man at Waterloo to let me examine it without the superior authority of the Yard. Even then he's such a stickler for rules and regulations that he will demand the authority of his own immediate superior."

"Very well," said Richardson, "he shall have all the authority that he wants."

"It will mean your going personally to Waterloo Station, sir," objected Lawrence.

"Oh, we can get over that. I'll give you a written authority to examine the package in the presence of the railway officials without taking it away. They will surely not object to that."

"But supposing it's a locked suitcase, sir. Are we to force the lock?"

"No, take Rawlings with you: he's got the proper outfit for a job of this sort and what he doesn't know about modern locks…"

"Very good, sir," said Lawrence. "Then I'll take with me the written authority in official form and start off with Mr Spofforth and Rawlings immediately."

They traversed the journey from Scotland Yard to Waterloo on foot; the pedestrian traffic was too thick to allow conversation and Spofforth was free to review his own position. He reflected that the parcel deposited in the cloakroom might turn out to contain nothing but underclothing; in that case he would not have added to his reputation by making a fuss about a trifle. On the other hand, should a search of this package produce important evidence his reputation would be made.

On arriving at the station it became clear that Lawrence not only knew his way about but had a friendly acquaintance with the men on the floor upstairs. He wasted no time in going to the cloakroom, but, leaving Spofforth and Rawlings on the wide platform below, he ran up the stairs to the room of one of his acquaintances, who rose to shake hands with him.

"I'm very glad to see you, Mr Lawrence. It's some time since you had occasion to pay us a visit. What can I do for you?"

Lawrence explained his business.

"Oh, that's a very simple matter," said Mr Cummings. "In fact I can do it off my own bat. You don't want to carry the package away but only to see what's in it?"

"Yes, but if it contains anything in the way of evidence for us I shall want you to hold it and not give it up to the depositor until you hear from us again."

"Very good; that shall be done. You say you have the number and date of the deposit receipt?"

"Yes, here it is."

"I'd better come down with you. We're a bit short-handed at this season and I can't get the cloakroom man to come here, but we shall be quite private at the back of the office down there."

They made their way to the cloakroom and entered it by a side door at the bottom of the stairs. Mr Cummings called, "Somers," and the principal cloakroom attendant came forward. "We want to have a look at a package deposited under this number. This gentleman comes from the Yard. You might bring the package round to the back where we shall be private."

Somers went to a shelf above their heads and descended the stepladder with a suitcase.

"It's locked," said Cummings. "I don't like to force it open."

"Oh, that's all right. I'll fetch my colleagues: one of them is an expert at this kind of job."

He went out and beckoned to the two men standing on the platform outside. "It's a suitcase," he explained, "and it's locked, but I suppose that little fact won't stand in your way, Rawlings."

"No sir. I've never yet met a suitcase that would baffle me. Ah! That's it, is it?" He examined the two locks and clicked his tongue. First he tried half-a-dozen keys from his bunch but failed to stir the lock. "Of course," he observed, "there's no difficulty, but I don't want to leave any marks behind me if I can help it—otherwise this gentleman will be getting an impassioned letter of complaint. 'Gently does it' is my motto and that of all competent luggage thieves."

While he was talking his fingers were busy with the locks and in a moment or two he was able to snap back the catches and throw the suitcase open. "There we are, sir," he said in the intonation of a conjuror when he has brought off a trick.

Spofforth found it difficult to control himself when the lid was thrown back, but in truth to the others the contents were disappointing—nothing but a neat parcel tied with string with at least a dozen knots and legibly addressed to "M. Henri, Rue Royale, Paris."

"We'll have to open this parcel," said Spofforth, pulling out a pocket knife.

"Steady," interjected Lawrence. "We've got to do the parcel up again without a sign that it has been tampered with. Don't cut the string: we must undo all those knots."

"Lord! That 'll take us half the morning."

"Not a bit of it; a little patience and what the newspapers call a 'blunt instrument' is all we want."

Rawlings' dexterous fingers solved the problem. In an incredibly short time he was unfolding the paper wrappings and disclosing the contents, which caused Spofforth to leap into the air with excitement: it was a lady's coat of mink fur.

Chapter Twenty

SPOFFORTH AWOKE the curiosity of Mr Cummings. "So this is what you were looking for?" he said.

"Yes, and it may prove to be the first step up the ladder to the gallows," said Lawrence grimly.

"Of course you'll take this coat to the Yard with you?" said Spofforth.

"No. We'll leave it here if Mr Cummings will arrange to telephone to me at the Yard as soon as the ticket is presented and in the meantime leave the depositor to wait and cool his heels."

"Certainly; that shall be arranged," said Cummings.

"And now we will tie that parcel up much as it was before and ask Rawlings to get to work with that patent tool of his and lock it up."

The three men returned to the Yard together and Lawrence and Spofforth went straight to Richardson's room to report what they had discovered.

Richardson listened thoughtfully and then said, "This is a case which calls for direct action, as the Labour leaders term it. We will send a polite invitation to Huskisson to call here on a matter which will interest him."

"Shall I take the message, sir?" asked Spofforth.

"No," said Richardson decidedly. "What you have to do is to resume your duties at Scudamore Hall as if nothing had occurred to interrupt them. We will attend to the rest of the business. Above all, not a hint of any kind to Mr Forge."

"Very good, sir," said Spofforth resignedly. He was dejected at the thought that he would now be debarred from swanking to Mr Forge of the great discovery that he had made; but orders were orders...

When Spofforth had left the room Richardson indicated his retreating figure with the blunt end of his pen. "There goes a most trustworthy man, Mr Lawrence, but trustworthiness is not everything that is wanted in our job. However, if he's done no more than track that mink coat into a cloakroom he's been worth his salt. After all, the service requires more than two sorts of men and a service composed of nothing but super-sleuths would let the country down in every direction. We need a strong leaven of the mediocre person who obeys orders and is content to use such brains as have been served out to him by his Maker. Our friend won't go very far in his profession, but he won't let us down."

"If this coat proves Huskisson to have been the murderer," said Lawrence, "we shall all be thinking of the public money thrown away in letting Dallas chase all over France to find in the end that the man he has been chasing has no graver charge to answer than one of dangerous driving."

"Quite so," nodded Richardson; "but those are risks that we have to take every day. We should get nowhere if we hesitated to take them. And now we must see about getting our friend Huskisson down to face the music."

"Yes sir. It's a fishing excursion and he may turn out to be a very wary old fish."

"Never mind; I have at my right hand a very wary old fisherman. You had better take on the job yourself, Mr Lawrence, and I won't ask how you did it."

Lawrence left the room chuckling at the compliment and swearing to himself that he could ask nothing better than to serve so generous a chief as Richardson. One thing was clear. Nothing must be done to alarm Huskisson since, if he were to destroy that cloakroom ticket, all their labour would be brought to nought. And yet how could he be inveigled into visiting the Yard without arousing his suspicion? Perhaps the straightforward way would prove in the end to be the best.

Chance played into Lawrence's hand when he reached the drive at Scudamore Hall and saw Huskisson making for the garage. He quickened his pace until he was within speaking distance of the retreating figure.

"Excuse me, Mr Huskisson," he called out. "Can I have a word with you?"

"As many as you like."

Lawrence thumped his chest in his endeavour to recover his wind.

"Well, sir, I've just come from the Yard. Information has reached us concerning the late Miss Gask which we think that you will be able either to corroborate or deny. Will you be kind enough to accompany me to the Yard and see Chief Constable Richardson? I have my car here and it can bring you back after the interview."

"Very good. I'm always glad to assist the police in any direction that I can, but I can't imagine what this new information can be."

"I'm afraid I'm not in a position to enlighten you."

During the drive Lawrence's attempts at cheerful conversation fell upon deaf ears. He could get nothing out of his passenger, not even an endorsement of his strictures upon the inclemency of the weather.

"Now, sir," he said as they pulled up at the main entrance to the famous building, "I think we will go straight up to the chief constable's room. We may have the luck to find him disengaged."

Richardson, as they learned from his messenger, was disengaged at the moment and they went straight in.

"I've brought Mr Huskisson with me, sir," said Lawrence. "I think you have some questions to ask him."

Richardson rose from his chair, shook hands with his visitor and indicated a padded armchair opposite to his table. "Sit down, Mr Huskisson. You must be cold after your drive. Mr Lawrence, no doubt, told you why we want to see you."

"I told him, sir," interjected Lawrence hastily, "that we wanted him to corroborate or to refute information that had come to us about the late Miss Gask, but I gave him no details."

"Those are soon given," said Richardson. He paused a moment and then said, "We have had information about that unfortunate lady which is not entirely to her credit. In plain language, did you know that she was mixed up in several very undesirable transactions?"

"The lady is dead and I would rather not discuss her character."

"I'm sorry to press my question, but I should not do so unless it were necessary. We know now that the emerald stolen from Mr Forge was passed by her into the hands of a receiver well known to the police, in Crooked Lane on the night of her death. The emerald was purchased by Mr Forge from the Marquis de Crémont, who had been introduced to Mr Forge by you. We feel it only fair to you to ask for any explanation you may be able to give. I may add that the Marquis de Crémont is now in prison in France; he has been implicated in jewel robberies to an astonishing amount." Richardson was quick to notice the look of concern upon his visitor's face and he took advantage of it. "I can see that this is news to you, but that it was not altogether unexpected. I suggest to you that your wisest course will be to lay all your cards on the table and withhold nothing."

"Are you trying to insinuate that I knew the character of this so-called marquis?"

"That is what we would like you to tell us," said Richardson with gentle gravity.

"Well, I can tell you this much. When I introduced him to Mr Forge all I knew about him was that he was a French aristocrat in need of funds and was anxious to sell the family heirlooms."

"Did you know of the connection between him and Miss Gask?"

"At that time I knew nothing."

"But afterwards?" insisted Richardson.

"Oh, afterwards I may have guessed."

"In fact you *did* guess."

"I see what you are trying to foist upon me—an admission that I was an accessory after the fact."

A solution of some of the evidence he had read at the beginning of the case flashed across Richardson's brain. He leaned forward towards his visitor and said, "Is it not a fact that on the morning of Miss Gask's death you were with her in the library at Scudamore Hall and you were struggling with her for possession of that emerald?" Huskisson changed colour.

"You seem to know a great deal about what went on. I did try to retrieve from Margaret Gask the emerald belonging to Mr Forge. I wished to restore it to its owner."

"You knew that she had stolen it?"

"Yes. Inadvertently she had let it fall from her handkerchief in which it had been rolled."

"I see. And let me ask you this. Did you follow her into Crooked Lane that evening and make another attempt to recover it?"

"Most certainly not."

Richardson looked at him fixedly for at least half a minute before putting his next question and Richardson's gaze had always proved to be extremely disconcerting to persons who had anything to hide.

"What was in that suitcase that you deposited at the cloakroom in Waterloo Station on the day following Miss Gask's murder?"

The question was so disconcerting that Huskisson wilted. "That's my business."

"Not altogether, I think. It may turn out to concern us also and that is why I'm questioning you."

"I've sometimes wondered whether you policemen come across anything that you regard as not being your business; but the contents of that suitcase belong to a friend of mine in Paris and I intend to restore them to their proper owner."

"In that case I am sure that you will have no objection to our seeing the contents before they go over to Paris. Have you the ticket in your pocket?"

At this point Huskisson lost his temper. "This is a bit too thick. You knew all along what was in that suitcase and I'll even bet that you've had it unlocked by some damned locksmith." He felt in his waistcoat pocket, produced the cloakroom ticket and flung it on the table. "There, that's the ticket and you can do your damnedest."

Richardson made the soft answer that turneth away wrath. "This will save us all a lot of trouble, Mr Huskisson. Mr Lawrence will take the ticket to Waterloo himself and bring back the suitcase. Would you care to go with him, or would you prefer to wait here until he arrives?"

"I've a telegram to send. I suppose I'm not under arrest?"

"Oh no, certainly not; but we should like you to be here when the suitcase is brought in order that you may unlock it in our presence. You'll find the telegraph office quite close to the bottom of the stairs."

"Very well. I'll be back in twenty minutes."

"I shall be back by then," said Lawrence, making for the stairs.

Left to himself, Richardson rang for his chief clerk of the C.I.D. Registry. "I want the file of that murder case in Surrey."

"You mean the Gask case, sir?"

"Yes; it ought to be on my table."

"The registry wanted it to add a paper that has come in from the Surrey chief constable."

"An important paper?"

"No sir; it is merely that they have traced another transaction between Margaret Gask and Fredman."

"Good. Let me have the file now: I want to refresh my memory."

As soon as it was brought Richardson set himself to read all the earlier papers connected with the case. He was thus engaged when Lawrence returned with the suitcase, closely followed by Huskisson.

"Ah! Is that the suitcase? I suppose you have the key with you, Mr Huskisson?"

"Yes, and I suppose that you will not take my word for what it contains. Policemen never do believe what they are told, I understand."

"That depends," said Richardson in his most soothing manner. "But I feel sure that it will be a relief to you to lay all your cards on the table rather than ask us to take anything for granted."

"Well, there are the keys," Huskisson said, throwing a couple of keys on the table. "You're not going to ask me to stand by while you perform your famous act of astonishment at the contents because I know that you've searched it already."

Meanwhile Lawrence was unlocking the suitcase and taking out the parcel it contained. He examined the knots. "It's very nicely tied up; it seems a pity to cut the string."

Huskisson took a penknife from his pocket and ruthlessly cut the string in several places. Lawrence detached the paper wrapping disclosing the fur coat.

"This coat belonged to Miss Gask, I believe," said Richardson quietly.

"It belongs to Monsieur Henri in Paris. You can read the address for yourself."

"You know that Miss Gask was believed to be wearing this coat on the night she was murdered."

"That is a good instance of the way in which you policemen jump to false conclusions. That parcel was tied up by me on the morning before Miss Gask's death."

Chapter Twenty-One

RICHARDSON ROSE from his chair and spread the fur coat with the fur upwards on the table under the window.

"I'm no expert in furs," he said, "but I imagine that a mink coat like this is worth a great deal of money."

"It is," said Huskisson shortly.

"Anything up to a thousand pounds, shall we say?"

"Probably."

"You have, of course, no objection to telling us how it came into your possession."

"I'm going to tell you the truth but with the full knowledge that you won't believe what I tell you. That coat was in the possession of Miss Gask. From information I had received in Paris I knew that a valuable mink coat had been stolen from Monsieur Henri, of the Rue Royale. I taxed Miss Gask with the theft. At first she assured me that it had been entrusted to her to take to England and effect a sale if possible. I needn't go into details, but in the end I managed to frighten her into consenting to let me return the coat anonymously to Monsieur Henri, its proper owner. But before I had had time to send it off to Paris she was murdered and there was a hue and cry about the coat."

"You could still have sent it anonymously to Monsieur Henri."

"I meant to, but I didn't want to get mixed up in any way with the murder and so I decided to leave the suitcase in the cloakroom until the fuss had died down."

"Weren't you afraid of being charged with being an accessory after the fact in the theft of the coat?"

Huskisson shrugged his shoulders. "There was of course that danger, and there was also the danger that I might be charged with her murder, as you police were so sure that she was wearing the coat that night."

Richardson smiled. "You had forgotten one thing that we should have looked for in relation to that coat."

"What was that?"

"Bloodstains."

"I see; the absence of bloodstains might absolve me from the suspicion of being her murderer, but it would leave me still open to suspicion of complicity in the theft."

"That's a question for Monsieur Henri and the French police. The coat was stolen from Monsieur Henri's premises and it has been found in your possession. Naturally you will have to account for how it got there. The coat will have to remain in our possession for the present and we shall have to inform the French authorities."

"I have already sent a telegram to a lady who is employed in Monsieur Henri's establishment, asking her to come over."

"You mean Mademoiselle Coulon?"

"Yes. I don't know how you got the name, but that's the lady: she will be able to identify the coat."

Richardson wondered whether Huskisson knew what Mlle Coulon's real business was. He threw out a feeler. "Is she one of the mannequins?"

"I believe she's a buyer. She knew Margaret Gask."

"Well, Mr Huskisson, I don't know that we need detain you any longer; but I must insist on the condition that if you leave Scudamore Hall you will notify us."

"I have no intention of leaving Scudamore Hall while Mr Forge is good enough to give me hospitality. I wish you good morning."

When the door was shut behind him Richardson said, "That's a good instance of the way in which we are handicapped. If that man had come forward and told the truth about this coat at the very beginning it might have made a difference."

"I don't know about that, sir. Of course we've had the trouble of trying to trace the coat..."

"Don't forget why we thought that she must have been wearing the coat. It was a very cold night and her body was found clad only in evening dress without any kind of covering—found with a bullet through the head. I am still of the opinion that she was wearing some outer covering for warmth and that outer covering for some reason was carried off by her murderer."

"I think that the explanation of Huskisson's behaviour is simple: he was in league with the woman over her thieving operations in Paris."

"That is not my view," said Richardson quietly. "I think that Huskisson had a real regard for Miss Gask and that it was a shock to him to find out that she was nothing more than a common thief; that his motive was to shield her good name."

Lawrence wilted. He had so profound a belief in his chief's acumen that his only reply was, "Then we're no nearer the real murderer."

"There's only one thing that puzzles me about the man. One would have thought that he had had enough of Scudamore Hall to last a lifetime, but you saw how ready he was to stay on there."

"Yes sir, I noticed that. I wonder whether he has got something hidden there…"

"If so, I suppose that we must trust Spofforth to find it out. Meanwhile a report of the finding of this coat must go to Dallas at once."

"Very good, sir; then I'll have a copy made. There should be a report from Dallas himself soon."

"I hope so. While you are getting that off to him you might send with it a good French version that he can hand straight to the French commissaire. Let them go over it carefully for accuracy in translation."

"Very good, sir. Minehead's French is good, but there is a man in the Special Branch whose French is as good as any Frenchman's. I'll get him to go over the report for possible blunders."

As soon as he was alone Richardson picked up the file of the Margaret Gask case to read the fresh report from the Kingston constabulary which his clerk had referred to. It described how in searching the premises of Fredman they had come across a letter signed by Margaret Gask and addressed from Paris. A copy of the letter was attached; Richardson read it carefully.

> *"7, Avenue Victor Emmanuel,*
> *"Paris.*

"I have received the notes you sent me. I can only say that I think the amount is scandalous. It does not encourage me to deal with you. Each of the pearls I sent you was worth that sum and I sent you thirty. Did A.G. deliver them all? Let me know that.

> "Margaret Gask"

"A.G.," thought Richardson, must be Arthur Graves. The French police had got him for the moment in safe custody. This little gang had worked together; obviously the small fry like Graves and Gask had not made much. Fredman's money was in process of being traced; it had been cunningly dispersed among several banks both French and English, but the total when it came to be reckoned up was likely to be staggering. Such a gang would not have worked at haphazard: at its head must have been a very competent leader. Certainly there was the Marquis de Crémont, but in Richardson's opinion it was certain that there must have been some Englishman working with him. The more he thought things over, the more convinced he was that James Oborn must be laid by the heels; but he had fled the country and Dallas might not have the luck to overtake him. For the moment, at any rate, he did not think that Douglas Oborn should again be questioned. There was Spofforth's report that the butler at Scudamore Hall had some kind of confidential relations with Douglas Oborn: Curtis was just the type of man to have been used as one of the smaller fry in the gang; it might well be that he was blackmailing Douglas Oborn on account of what he knew about his brother. The moment might come for questioning Curtis, but it had not come yet; it was important not to arouse any suspicion that the gang was in process of being rounded up.

The report from the Salisbury police had not yet reached him, though it might be floating around the office. He rang and made enquiries about it.

"It ought to be on Mr Lawrence's table, sir," said the clerk. "The registry received it this morning and at once marked it 'pressing' because we knew that you were waiting for it. I'll enquire, sir."

Lawrence himself entered with the report in his hand. "I have only just had time to read this, sir, on account of that business in Waterloo Station."

"What is the gist of it? I haven't time to go through it at this moment."

"Well, sir, there's nothing criminal known against James or Douglas Oborn. Apparently the family was not united. The mother and the two eldest sons were Roman Catholics and the youngest son, Charles, was brought up in his father's faith as a member of the Church of England. For this reason they had little in common with one another. When the mother died it was found that she had left her money to James and Douglas and the father, who died a year later, left the whole of his money and his practice to Charles. Since the father's funeral neither of the two elder brothers has been seen in Salisbury. It is common gossip among those who knew them that there was a violent quarrel between them and Charles."

"There's nothing much to help us in that."

"No sir; everything might be different if Dallas succeeds in tracing James. Both Arthur Graves and Margaret Gask knew James Oborn, but apparently Douglas was unknown to any of them."

The telephone bell on Richardson's desk rang. He picked up the receiver and made the usual replies that began with affirmatives, "yes"—"yes"—"yes." He listened attentively for a moment and then said, "Hang on a moment," and put the palm of his hand over the instrument. "It's from Huskisson," he hissed to Lawrence. "He's had a message from Mademoiselle Coulon to say that she is leaving Paris by air this afternoon."

"You would like me to meet her, sir?"

"Huskisson says that he'll meet her at Croydon and that he'd like you to go with him. I suppose he doesn't want us to think that he wants a private conversation with her first."

"Very good, sir; I'll go."

"He says he'll call for you in his car." Richardson used the telephone again. "Mr Lawrence will be ready if you call here on your way." He put down the receiver.

"Do you think that Huskisson knows that this lady is employed by the French police, sir?"

"From his replies to my questions I gathered that he did not. Put this coat back in the suitcase and lock it up until she comes."

"Have you been through the pockets, sir?"

"No. As it belongs to that French firm and was stolen in Paris, we won't touch it before we hand it over. She can do the searching."

Lawrence glanced at the clock. "Mr Huskisson will soon be here if we are to get to Croydon to meet the airplane. I have several things to dispose of before I can start, so if you'll excuse me..."

"You need not trouble to bring him to me before you start, of course. I shall be here quite late this evening with all this mass of work before me."

Richardson was so much engrossed in his work that he lost all count of time. He looked up in astonishment when his messenger came in to announce that Superintendent Lawrence and a lady were in the waiting room.

"Ask them to come in at once."

Pauline Coulon looked none the worse for her flight from Le Bourget. She glanced curiously round the room and then fixed her grey eyes on Richardson.

"I am very glad to meet the gentleman of whom I have heard so much," she said as she shook hands, "and also to see your famous Scotland Yard."

Richardson responded in the same tone. "I am delighted to meet yet another member of the service in which I have so many friends. Now, to work! Mr Lawrence, will you bring in that fur coat for Mademoiselle Coulon to see?"

As soon as the door had closed behind Lawrence she said, "So Spofforth did find that cloakroom ticket after all."

Chapter Twenty-Two

RICHARDSON SHOWED no surprise at her question. "You did not expect him to?"

"When I was at Scudamore Hall and had an opportunity of observing him I did not think—how shall I put it—that he belonged to the first choice in the market. But of course I had more intimate knowledge of the people concerned in the business than he had…"

"Do you mean," asked Richardson, "that you suspected Mr Huskisson of having that coat in his possession?"

"Short of legal proof I felt sure of it. I knew that it was a great shock to Monsieur Huskisson when he learned that Margaret Gask had been a professional thief. I had told him in Paris of the loss of that coat by the firm of Henri. In a conversation I had with him at Scudamore Hall I realised that he knew that she had not been wearing that coat on the night of her death. While I was there I managed to engage in a little searching and was able to convince myself that it was not in the house. I had noticed a little habit of Monsieur Huskisson of slipping his fingers into the top pocket of his waistcoat as if to assure himself that something was still there. This prompted me to take the first opportunity of searching that pocket and it was thus that I found the cloakroom ticket from Waterloo."

"What I find difficult to understand, mademoiselle, is that you should have quitted the country without trying to obtain possession of the coat, which, after all, was the property of your employers. It was surely the object of your quest in England."

"It was." She paused a moment and then proceeded to pick her words slowly and carefully. "I came to the conclusion that poor Margaret Gask was only a tool in the hands of more important people. I felt sure that she had met her death at the hands of one of these. The hue and cry for the fur coat was likely to lull the murderer into a false security, as he would know that she was not wearing it on the night of her death. I therefore decided to let the investigations go on a little further before I showed my hand."

"I see. As we are both engaged in the same investigation, let me ask you one question. Have you any reason for suspecting Mr Huskisson of being concerned in any way in the activities of these people?"

"Certainly not," she said decidedly. "The strictest investigations have been made recently and nothing has been found against him."

Lawrence entered with the suitcase in his hand. He placed it on the table and opened it, disclosing the coat. Mlle Coulon jumped up and took it out. She passed her hand almost reverently over the fur and said, "There is no possible doubt: this is the coat."

"No doubt Monsieur Henri will be able to prove this beyond dispute," said Richardson.

"Certainly, monsieur; but stop! You can prove it for yourself. If you undo the lining you will find Revillon's initials, E.R., stamped on every skin. Not only can Monsieur Henri prove it but Monsieur Revillon himself. But first will you permit me to feel in the pockets?"

"Certainly. We have not yet done so."

With deft fingers Pauline Coulon explored the pockets which were in the lining of the coat. She brought out a visiting card and read the inscription aloud. "'Monsieur Salmond, Boulevard des Invalides.'"

"I have heard that name before," said Richardson. "It has figured in the reports of my agent in Paris."

"Ah yes! Monsieur Dallas. He and Monsieur Goron together will clear up this case, I promise you. See what is written in the corner of this card. 'Always at home after 8 P.M.' This may seem a small thing, but it may turn out to be very important for us. It proves that Miss Gask knew Monsieur Salmond."

"I believe that Monsieur Goron has a theory about that," said Richardson.

"He has. And now I would like to ask Mr Huskisson one or two questions. Is he still waiting downstairs?"

"Yes," said Lawrence. "I left him to wait until we called him. I'll fetch him."

"Is it your wish to see him alone?" asked Richardson. "Not at all, provided that you say nothing that will cause him to tighten those thin lips of his."

"Have no fear. It is not the first time that I have had to put questions to reluctant witnesses."

At this point Lawrence ushered Huskisson into the room. Richardson motioned him to a chair.

"Now that we're all together," he said pleasantly, "Mademoiselle would like to ask you one or two questions."

"Go ahead, Pauline," said Huskisson with a readiness that surprised Richardson, who had hitherto seen him only in aggressive or defensive moods.

"The coat has been found, my friend. There is no longer any concealment necessary over that. So much is known about poor Margaret now that it is useless for you and me to defend her character. All we can do is to help in bringing her murderer to justice."

"That devil shall be found," said Huskisson through his clenched teeth.

Pauline Coulon turned to Richardson. "Voila! You see that we have an ally, not an antagonist."

"I am very pleased to see it," said Richardson. "I'm glad that Mr Huskisson no longer regards us as his natural enemies."

"And I hope," retorted Huskisson, "that the police no longer regard me as the murderer of Miss Gask whom they have to bring to justice."

"Now," said Pauline, drawing her chair a few inches nearer to the table, "this is my first question. Did you ever hear Margaret speak of Monsieur Salmond?"

"You mean the senator who was murdered last November? Yes, I once saw her dining with him at the Boeuf sur le Toit."

"You were not pleased?" suggested Pauline gently.

"I was not," he agreed, "but she told me that she had been hoping to get him to help her in establishing a dressmaking business, which was difficult at that time for a foreigner."

"Can you tell me how she took the news of his death?" Huskisson hesitated a moment and Pauline added, "She took it badly, no doubt?"

"Yes. I may as well tell you what happened. I met her at the Café Veil for an *apéritif* and I had just bought a paper. I opened it and found on the front page in big type, 'A Senator Found Dead. Was It Murder?' Margaret snatched the paper from my hand, saying, 'What is his name?' When she read Monsieur Salmond's name she was very much upset."

Richardson interposed a question. "In thinking it over quietly would you say that her agitation was no more than you would expect her to show at the loss of an influential friend?"

"In thinking it over now I should say that her agitation was due to terror."

An exclamation of satisfaction escaped from Pauline.

"I must lose no time in getting back to Paris to put Monsieur Goron in possession of these new facts."

"You can't go back tonight," said Huskisson; "it's too late."

Pauline wrinkled her forehead in thought. "Perhaps I might ask Mr Forge to give me hospitality for the night and let me catch the first plane from Croydon tomorrow morning."

"I'm sure he would be delighted. I'll go out and telephone to him. I have my car here and could drive you down to Scudamore Hall."

When Huskisson had gone Richardson said with a smile, "Your visit, mademoiselle, has had one useful result. It has removed one of our suspects from the list."

"Ah, that poor Monsieur Huskisson. He is his own enemy. Unfortunately my chief, Monsieur Goron, in Paris suspects him also and it is a serious matter for those who have drawn Monsieur Goron's suspicions to themselves."

"Nevertheless," said Richardson, "having seen that fur coat, it is clear to me that she was not wearing it when she was murdered—otherwise there must have been bloodstains and there are none. Therefore we need not detain the coat."

While he was speaking Pauline's deft fingers had been busy in detaching the lining from the fur; she disclosed the back of three or four skins and showed that each had stamped upon it the initials E.R.

"There is my proof, monsieur, and if you will allow me I will take it back to Paris with me and return it to Monsieur Henri. Having recovered it, you understand, will be what you say in English 'a feather in my cap.'"

A knock at the door announced the return of Huskisson.

"I've telephoned to Mr Forge and he was beside himself with pleasure at the thought of entertaining you again."

"I'm ready," she said, "and if you will lend me your suitcase we'll take the coat with us to Scudamore Hall, so that I shall not have the delay of fetching it in the morning."

"If you get any further information," said Richardson as they shook hands, "you will of course pass it on to us through Mr Dallas."

"That shall be done, monsieur, and I shall also let you know how Monsieur Henri behaves when his property is unexpectedly restored to him. His transports of joy will be worth recording."

As she took her seat in the car beside Huskisson she said, "Did I not tell you, my friend, that your police were mistaken in thinking that when they found that fur coat they would have found the murderer?"

"You did, and I wondered then how much you knew and how you came to know it."

"Ah! I mustn't give away the secrets of my profession. But do tell me why you are continuing to stay with Mr Forge."

"Well, I realised that the police would follow me wherever I went; also Forge likes to have me and he's rather a decent sort."

"And one more reason?"

"Well," he admitted reluctantly, "there is another reason. I can't help thinking that in that house we shall find the clue to Margaret's murderer and I won't rest until he's been brought to justice."

"Do you mean that you are carrying on private detective work?"

"Not that exactly, but I'm searching for a revolver or a blood-stained wrap of some kind."

"But surely the police have searched the place thoroughly?"

"The police have searched the lane and the neighbourhood thoroughly for the revolver; I am searching inside the grounds."

"Do you suspect a member of the household?"

"Well, I've really no grounds for suspicion, beyond the fact that I don't trust the butler."

"The butler? You mean the good Curtis?"

"Well, I'll tell you one thing that I saw. On the morning when I was going to take this suitcase to the cloakroom at Waterloo Station I got up early and took it to the garage before I thought anyone would be about. The garage door was locked, but I knew that the key was kept hanging on a nail in one of the sheds close by. There is a loft in this shed which is reached by a removable ladder. I saw the butler dragging a tin suitcase after him up the ladder. There is nothing suspicious about that, you will say, but there was something suspicious about his manner when he saw me."

"In what way?"

"Well, he looked disturbed and he entered into quite unnecessary explanations as to why he was taking the box up to the loft."

"What did he say?"

"Oh, that the lumber room in the house was getting chock-a-block with empty trunks and he was moving some of them. Since then I've made it my business to go up the ladder and I found that the loft was empty except for that one trunk, which is locked. Although it is not very heavy I'm sure that it contains something and that it wasn't empty, as he said it was."

"You didn't think that what you saw was important enough to report to the police?"

"No; I didn't want to look a fool. I made up my mind somehow or other to find out what the trunk contained, but so far I haven't had the chance."

"If I were staying long enough I think I could find a way. It would be good fun to see the face of that butler." The car swung through a gate. "What, are we here already?"

"Yes; I'll drive you up to the front door in style and then take the car across to the garage."

"I will study well the countenance of the butler when he opens the door to me," said Pauline as she sprang lightly out.

But it was not the butler who responded to the front doorbell. It was Spofforth, who was closely followed by Mr Forge.

"Oh, mademoiselle," said her host, "I thought you were the doctor. I am delighted to see you again, but at the moment we are rather upset. There has been an accident and I telephoned for the doctor."

"An accident?"

"Yes; my butler has fallen from the loft to the cement floor of the shed and we are afraid that he is rather badly injured."

Chapter Twenty-Three

THERE ARE ALWAYS ups and downs in the business of detection and Richardson had spent a restless night in thinking over the day's work that lay behind him. He had not covered himself with glory. Perhaps it was because he had allowed his mind to dwell too much upon details such as the recovery of that fur coat and too little on the real object of his quest—the murderer of Margaret Gask. After all, the discovery of that fur coat was only a link in the chain, an important link no doubt, but no more than a link. In the course of his broodings he fell asleep and woke late, a very unusual occurrence for him. He was a little later than usual in arriving at his office.

On his table lay a letter addressed to him personally in Dallas' handwriting and bearing the Paris postmark. He slit the envelope open with more impatience than was usual to him. The document it contained was long, but he read it with the concentration that he always brought to bear upon his most interesting cases.

"In spite of every effort made by M. Goron and the French Sûreté Generale I have to report that so far the Sûreté have been unable to trace the car that James Oborn took in exchange for his own from the garage at Montargis. This has puzzled the French authorities because the net has been spread to cover the entire country, including in particular the places on the coast from which cars are shipped as well as the various frontier posts of Switzerland, Spain, Belgium and Italy. The easiest method for baffling pursuit at one time would have been to traverse the Pyrenees into Spain by one of the least guarded passes, such as Dancheronea, but at present the whole of the Spanish frontier is closely guarded. This is not to say that particular frontier guards, military or civil, cannot be 'squared.' M. Goron clings to the theory that James Oborn is still in France."

The report broke off here and the remaining pages were dated a day later.

"We have been following a fresh clue. In a former report I said that the pearl necklace found on Arthur Graves was suspected of being one stolen from Mlle Saulnois, the actress, from her villa at Nice. She has now identified it definitely as being her property. At the time of her loss she was entertaining friends in her villa at Nice. All except one of these guests are still staying with her. This absent guest, who left her villa about a week after the robbery, was a priest who had escaped from a Spanish monastery on account of the civil war.

"Mlle Saulnois's theory is that a cat-burglar entered her room through the window while the necklace was lying on her dressing table. She was called away by a domestic contretemps that had arisen. Her cook was discovered drunk with the dinner only partly ready and she had to get it ready to be served by standing over the rest of the staff. In the kitchen crisis she forgot about her necklace and did not return to her bedroom until some hours later, when she discovered the loss. She immediately telephoned to the police who sent up Commissaire Ponchot, a very intelligent officer, who brought with him Brigadier Lammas to assist him in the enquiry. A new terrace was being built outside her bedroom and scaffold poles were lying about the wall; one of these had been propped against her window and the commissaire was convinced that this had been the mode of access. The staff had all been busy under the eyes of their mistress at the time and were, therefore, clear of suspicion. There had been an epidemic of these burglaries in the neighbourhood and in spite of the efforts of the police there had been no arrests.

"In view of Arthur Graves's statement that he had received the necklace from the Marquis de Crémont, M. Goron and I went together to the prison for a second interview with the marquis. For some time he stuck to his story that the jewels were heirlooms in his family, but when M. Goron pointed out that his sentence might be doubled for the theft of the necklace he changed his tune and declared that he would tell the truth. As is common in such cases, the story that he told is probably only part of the truth. He said that he bought the necklace from a Spanish priest who had escaped from a monastery in Spain. He readily gave the name of the man as Father Collet and also the name of the hotel at St Raphael in which they were both staying at the time of the transaction. He said that the priest was in such dire need of money that he offered the necklace for five thousand francs, a sum far below its real value and he added with a shrug of his shoulders, 'You will understand that I could not resist such a bargain.' Goron pressed him very hard in an attempt to get further information, but neither threats nor hints that he might obtain remission if he told the truth could induce him to enlarge any further on his story.

"On our way back from the prison, I passed on to M. Goron the information you sent me concerning James Oborn's early life—that he had been educated for the Roman Catholic priesthood. M. Goron at once rose to the bait. There must be some connection between that Spanish priest and James Oborn, he declared. Although in my opinion the connection seemed slight I consented to his proposal that we should take a fast police car and run down to the Riviera to make enquiries on the spot.

"We went first to the hotel at St Raphael and verified the fact that a Spanish monk who signed his name Père Collet had stayed there during the first week in November. He seemed to be much depressed at having, as he said, been turned out of his own country and was making for Switzerland. The hotel manager, an old acquaintance of M. Goron, gave us one interesting item of information. The Spanish monk could not speak or understand much of his own language. This was made clear by some other

Spaniards who were staying in his hotel and were anxious to enter into conversation with a fellow refugee, particularly as he belonged to a religious order. His French was fluent, but there was an unmistakable foreign accent in his pronunciation. We asked the manager whether it was possible that he was an Englishman posing as a Spaniard. He thought for a moment and then said yes, that was quite possible.

"We then asked the manager whether the Marquis de Crémont had been staying at the hotel at the same time. He turned over the pages of his registration book and said yes, he had stayed one day longer than the monk.

"M. Goron next enquired whether there was any monastery near at hand and was told that there was one near Fréjus. We held a private consultation and came to the conclusion that this monk and James Oborn might be one and the same person. As he had on that occasion assumed the disguise of a priest it seemed more than possible that he might be enjoying the hospitality of some monastery at the present moment. We decided to call on the monks at the St Augustin House.

"When we arrived there we were kept waiting a considerable time before we could have an interview with the abbot, but at last we were shown into a private room. When the abbot presented himself Goron went straight to the point, telling him that we were in search of an Englishman who was probably disguised as a Spanish monk. The abbot was not communicative: he said that we could get the information we required on application to the prefecture. Noticing our surprise, he said, 'Have you not heard of what occurred here yesterday? No?' He then told us that two days before an Englishman, who said that he was a refugee from Spain and that he was a monk but had escaped in civilian clothes, had begged hospitality for a few days. He had arrived in a motorcar. The day after his arrival a gendarme had called; he said that this car had been traced to the monastery and that the driver was wanted by the English police. The refugee, who had given the name of Collet, was sent for; but he strenuously denied that he was the man of whom the English were in search. The gendarme said that he must accompany him to the prefecture to clear himself before the préfet. One of the rules of the monastery was hospitality and the gendarme was invited to *déjeuner*. He accepted and during the meal the refugee was lodged in the serving room, with two brothers to act as guards at the door. There was no other exit from the serving room except through the dining room and yet after the meal it was found that he had disappeared. None of the brothers who served the meal could have connived at his escape.

"We questioned the abbot about the looks of the escaped man and he said that to all appearances he was what he professed to be; he was wearing sandals on bare feet and he was correctly tonsured.

"Being unable to get more information from the abbot, Goron decided to apply for an interview with the préfet. This official made no secret of the man's escape. He said that they had had a telegram from Paris requiring them to keep a lookout for a certain car and detain the driver. It had been traced to the monastery; a gendarme was sent with the result, which we already knew, that the man had escaped. He was able to tell us how the escape had been contrived. It was discovered afterwards that a white suit with cap of a cook's assistant was missing from the serving room. Evidently the prisoner had slipped on this disguise, seized a dish, walked through the dining room and out into the grounds and made good his escape. The gendarmerie were now hunting for him, but so far without result.

"We asked the préfet whether the car had been detained and whether the luggage of the escaped man had been taken from the monastery. He said that both had been done and that both were in the hands of the local gendarmerie. We went on to the gendarmerie and were received in friendly fashion by the local commandant, M. Lemare, who was very pleased to see M. Goron, his chief in Paris. He explained that he was at the moment preparing a report for him.

"In the car they had discovered a box containing a number of tools such as are used by expert burglars, together with a rope ladder with hooks at one end for attaching it to a balcony or window sill. There were no valuables or marks of identification of the owner of the tools. The few fingerprints found on the varnish were blurred. The luggage contained two ordinary lounge suits, in addition to underclothing with the maker's name, Burberry, Paris. There were no papers of any kind: any documents that he may have had must have been carried on his person.

"While we were there a gendarme came in, mounted on a motorcycle: he had been one of the party sent out to search the woods at Valescure. He had brought with him a priest's soutane which he had found rolled up behind the hedge bordering the road near Valescure. It bore no identification marks. M. Goron readily agreed with my suggestion that under his clerical garments the man was wearing ordinary civilian clothes: that would make his escape much easier, since the instructions to the gendarmerie had been to hunt for a man in clerical clothes. Provided that he had a sufficiency of funds, his escape would now be fairly easy, with the exception of one point—his tonsured head. That would certainly be an important point in identification; unobservant people might take the tonsure for ordinary baldness, but not the police who were pursuing the fugitive.

"I suggested to M. Goron that the first thing he would do would be to provide himself with socks, shoes and a hat. Goron agreed and said that to obtain these he would have to go to Cannes, and asked M. Lemare to have enquiries made at all men's clothiers.

"Having left these instructions, we decided that it would be useless for us to remain in the neighbourhood, since any incident in the pursuit would be telegraphed to Paris.

"On our return to Paris I decided to question Arthur Graves once more. I found him in a very depressed state of mind and he assured me that he would gladly give me information, but he knew nothing more than what he had already said. I asked him if he knew that James Oborn was a Roman Catholic priest. He remembered having been sent by James Oborn to the post office to fetch a letter which had been addressed poste restante. He gave him an identity card made out in the name of James Collet with the profession marked as priest. The letter was handed over without question by the official. Graves confessed that he was very curious about this letter, as James Oborn had seemed anxious to have it but seemed afraid to go and fetch it himself.

"This seems to confirm the fact that Collet and James Oborn are one and the same person. I was also able to get from Graves the information that James Oborn had landed in England from France at the end of November.

I shall not fail to report any further developments and I shall remain in Paris meanwhile.

"ALBERT DALLAS, *Detective Inspector*."

Chapter Twenty-Four

RICHARDSON FINISHED reading Dallas' report and sent immediately for Lawrence.

"Take this report, Mr Lawrence, and read it slowly and carefully; it comes from Detective Inspector Dallas and it is very important."

Lawrence pulled out his spectacle case and polished his glasses, then, standing with his back to the window, he began to read, while Richardson busied himself with the other papers on his desk. When he became aware that Lawrence was standing with his back to the window he said, "No, no; that's not the way. All important documents should be read while sitting: only in that position is the brain able to concentrate. Sit down."

Lawrence knew from experience his chief's idiosyncrasies and took the line of least resistance. He sat down to read; silence brooded over the room. At last the report had been read and digested; Lawrence indicated this by a fluttering of the pages.

"Well," said Richardson, "what do you make of it?"

"I think that if they capture James Oborn they will have the man we are all looking for."

"So do I."

There came a discreet knock on the door; Richardson's messenger appeared. "I'm sorry to interrupt you gentlemen," he said, "but the lady who was here yesterday, Mademoiselle Coulon, wants to see you on what she says is a very important matter. Mr Huskisson is with her."

"Very well; show them in. You had better sit tight, Mr Lawrence, and keep your ears open."

Pauline Coulon entered the room with the air of a bearer of strange tidings. She began at once.

"When I was here last evening, monsieur, I did not think that I should have to trouble you again so soon, but things have happened which we feel ought to be reported to you at once."

If she had expected that Richardson would be startled into curiosity she was disappointed. In an official life which consisted mainly of receiving shocks his nerves had been dulled into accepting the most startling news without tremor. Many of his subordinates deplored this attitude of mind.

"Go ahead; I'm listening," was all he said, though this did not prevent him from turning over papers while he listened.

"The first thing is that Curtis, the butler at Scudamore Hall, has had an accident. He fell from the loft to a cement floor in a shed attached to the garage and has been unconscious ever since. The doctor thinks his condition grave." Richardson nodded. "You think perhaps that that is not very important, but who shall say what may result from this accident?" She turned to Huskisson, saying, "Tell them about that little episode of the tin trunk."

Huskisson rather haltingly gave them an account of how he had seen Curtis dragging the trunk up to the loft.

"But," observed Richardson, "his excuse seemed reasonable. What are lofts used for but to store unwanted things?"

"The tin trunk is the only object in the loft. Do you not think that it should be opened and examined without Curtis' knowledge?"

Richardson turned to Lawrence. "In view of Curtis' criminal record, I think this might be done."

"I've had a look at the trunk," said Huskisson. "It has two locks and it looks as if it might require an expert locksmith. The man you took to Waterloo Station would be the very man for the job."

"Yes, Rawlings would be the man," said Richardson. "How came Curtis to fall?"

"He had to go up a movable ladder and apparently the ladder had slipped," explained Huskisson.

"I have put off my departure," said Pauline, "expressly to see this affair through. Mr Huskisson has his car down below and he could drive Mr Lawrence and your locksmith back with us to Scudamore Hall."

"Ah, but then we should have to get back again," said Lawrence. "I think that we had better take one of the police cars."

"Yes," said Richardson. "It will excite less remark than if you all arrived together. Try to arrange your expedition without all the servants crowding round as an audience."

"Mr Huskisson and I will go back first and prepare Mr Forge for your coming," said Pauline. "You will not have to come to the house at all, but drive straight to the outbuildings. Now, Mr Huskisson." She paused with her hand upon the doorknob and Huskisson followed her like a well-trained dog.

"I hope this is not going to turn out to be a wild-goose chase," said Richardson. "I'm not much of a believer in letting women mess about in detective work, but this young lady seems to have unusual gifts. We might do worse than give her her head."

"I'm glad to hear you say so," said Lawrence. "Since the war women have been butting in everywhere…"

"They have, and I suppose we must admit that most of them are making good. Now, you and Rawlings had better get off. There is nothing for us to do on this report and if anything comes of your visit to Scudamore Hall you will be able to send it off to Dallas."

Rawlings proved to be at liberty and three minutes later he and Lawrence were on their way. Rawlings was a man of few words and Lawrence found conversation a little heavy in hand. He began with the subject of the locks.

"I'm afraid that you'll have your work cut out with those locks, Mr Rawlings. I understand that it's a metal trunk with an unusual kind of lock."

"As long as the lock doesn't bite my fingers I'm not afraid of it," said Rawlings sardonically.

Lawrence laughed. "What an idea that would be for one of these mystery writers—a lock that bit the fingers of the lock-smith, with a concealed man trap inside."

"I could make you one of those if it would be of any use to the Yard," retorted Rawlings.

"I've no doubt you could. It would be a better burglar alarm than any now on the market."

After this exchange of ideas Rawlings was buried in silent thought. At last he gave tongue. "I've often thought," he said, "what the Yard might become if a little fresh blood were pumped into it."

"To my mind there are already too many changes. In the old days when detective officers were encouraged to know the men they had to deal with we got on a lot better. Now, here we are; this is the gate. If you'll hold it open for me we'll drive straight to the shed: I know the one they mean and you can have a look at those locks."

When they arrived at the door of the shed they found Mr Forge, Mlle Coulon and Huskisson waiting for them. Greetings having been exchanged, Forge assumed the leadership. To be leader of a band of experts filled his soul with satisfaction.

"This is the trunk," he said a little pompously. "I got Mr Huskisson to go up and bring it down to be all ready for you."

"Has your butler recovered consciousness yet?" enquired Lawrence.

"Yes, but the doctor has prescribed entire quiet. No one has been near him but the nurse and she won't allow him to be questioned."

"Where is your other guest?" Lawrence sunk his voice as he asked the question.

"Oh, he's up in London; he got a telegram from his brother, the lawyer in Salisbury, making an appointment."

Pauline turned to Lawrence, saying innocently, "Most convenient, wasn't it, Mr Lawrence?"

"Most convenient," agreed Lawrence, giving her a sharp look. In his mental rating of her she had scored another point.

Rawlings was kneeling in front of the box scrutinizing the locks. He pulled his leather tool bag towards him, took out a bunch of keys, tried the most likely one and whistled.

"These are rather special locks," he said, "and I'm not sure—"

"You're not going to tell us that you haven't brought the proper tools?" asked Forge testily.

"No, but it may take a little more time than I thought it would."

Three of his listeners looked perturbed, but not so Lawrence, who knew Rawlings' little weakness of old: no job on his showing was ever an easy one. He was careful to turn the locks away from his audience while he was tinkering with them, but a moment later Forge uttered an exclamation of triumph; Rawlings had performed the conjuring trick; the lid of the trunk gaped open.

Lawrence fell on his knees beside the trunk and began to explore the contents.

"I suppose it is perfectly well understood before we go any further that all this is to be strictly confidential and that not a word of it must be allowed to leak out. I say this because I shall have to take this trunk away with me to Scotland Yard."

He was looking at Mr Forge as he uttered this warning and the owner of Scudamore Hall drew himself up. "Not a word shall pass my lips, even to Spofforth."

"Of course," said Lawrence soothingly, "I knew that we could rely upon you, but if a word should get out we should have the reporters round us like bees after honey."

Forge shut his lips tight, perhaps as an indication of his future attitude to prying reporters.

"Now, Mr Lawrence," said Pauline impatiently, "you have all the assurance you want. Take the things out of the box and let us see them."

Lawrence hesitated. The Yard training to secrecy was strong.

"Surely you would not baulk a woman's curiosity so cruelly," pleaded Pauline.

With the air of a conjuror taking a rabbit from a hat he produced from the box a curious-looking garment in coarse brown material with a hood.

"*Tiens!*" exclaimed Pauline. "It's a monk's robe. Why should a butler have that?"

"Yes, why?" echoed Lawrence. "There are other things here belonging to a monk's outfit—a waist cord and a wig with a tonsure. What have we here?" He unwrapped a newspaper parcel. "Sandals. It is because this is such a peculiar kit for a butler that I shall have to take the box up to the yard."

Mr Forge looked disappointed: it seemed such a dull denouement to a drama that had started so promisingly.

Lawrence began to act. "Lock the box again, Rawlings, and help me carry it to the car. We mustn't waste any more time." Three minutes later the car was shooting down the hill.

"I shall get back to the house now and hear from the nurse how her patient is," said Forge fussily. "I wonder why the man was carrying about a monk's robe."

"Be sure you don't ask him that question," said Pauline warningly. "It would hamper Mr Lawrence very much if you did."

Forge turned an indignant face upon her. "Is it likely that I should? Besides, no one is allowed to go near him with that nurse on guard at the door."

"Well, I must say good-bye and thank you for your hospitality. I must be off and Mr Huskisson is kindly driving me to Croydon to catch the airplane."

"Good-bye," said Forge, shaking hands warmly. "I wish you were staying longer. Be sure that you regard this house as your hotel whenever you come to England."

Pauline laughed gaily. "Take care what you say, monsieur. I may be back here tomorrow if you're too pressing." She climbed into Huskisson's car. "You see I have my luggage all on board." She waved her hand in farewell as the car swung into the drive.

"What worries me," growled Huskisson as they turned into the main road, "is that that old man will never keep so good a story to himself. He's sure to blab; I'll bet you that Oborn hears the whole story at lunch."

"That would never do, as that suit probably belongs to his brother James. He'll be full of suspicion as soon as he finds out that the telegram signed with his brother Charles' name was a bogus one. You've got your work cut out. You'll have to shadow Mr Forge and not give him an opportunity of being alone with Oborn."

"I shall shadow Oborn too," said Huskisson grimly. "I'll see that he doesn't go prying into that loft."

"You think that he knew as well as the butler what was hidden in that trunk?"

"I do."

"If he finds out that it's gone he can't do much. It would be impossible for him to warn his brother, and mark my words, my friend," Pauline concluded impressively, "that James will be found within the next few hours."

Chapter Twenty-Five

SUPERINTENDENT LAWRENCE, with the assistance of Rawlings, carried the box into Richardson's room at Scotland Yard and as soon as the locksmith had left the room Lawrence opened it and displayed the contents.

"Rather a strange garb for a butler to be carrying about, don't you think, sir?" he asked.

"Very," agreed his chief; "but I've seen stranger disguises in my time."

"In view of the fact that James Oborn adopts this disguise and that Spofforth suspects there to be a secret understanding between Curtis and Douglas Oborn, this may prove to be important evidence."

Richardson picked up a report lying on his table and said, "While you have been away this has come in from the Salisbury police: they have discovered that Curtis was at one time employed by the Oborn family."

"I wish we had some reason for holding Douglas Oborn," said Lawrence. "He is bound to be suspicious, as Mademoiselle Coulon sent him a forged telegram to get him out of the way and he may have gone to the post office for information about the sender."

"The danger is that he may know all the secret hiding places of his brother and warn him; but we must risk that."

"He can't get out of the country himself because we've put up the gate against him. The butler, I'm afraid, won't be fit to be questioned just yet."

"I suppose he was already getting jumpy and had gone to the loft to move either the trunk or its contents to another hiding place. I thought that it wouldn't be a bad thing for it to leak out among the staff below stairs that Spofforth was a detective. When people get suspicious and nervy they are apt to give themselves away."

"This accident may prove to be a lucky thing for us," said Lawrence. "I haven't searched this garment, sir."

Richardson took up the robe and began to look it over. "What an extraordinary number of pockets! Mostly empty, I'm afraid," he said as he plunged his hand into each one. His fingers came into contact with a paper which rustled. He drew out a bank note and spread it out on the table. "This is a French note for five thousand francs, stamped by the Credit Lyonnais in Paris." He was plunged in thought for a few moments and Lawrence forbore to interrupt him. "You remember," he said at last, "that senator who was murdered in Paris. What was his name? Salmond. It was discovered at the police enquiry that he had been robbed of several thousand franc notes. I wonder whether this was one of them and whether the assassin left it because he thought it might be risky to change it on account of its being stamped."

Lawrence did not answer immediately. He had picked up the paper in which the sandals had been wrapped and was scrutinizing it, especially where a piece had been torn off. "And, if I remember rightly, sir, another clue that Monsieur Goron had in that case was a strip of paper taken from the continental edition of the *Daily Mail*."

"You are right," said Richardson. "These things ought to be sent to Monsieur Goron at once. Has Mademoiselle Coulon left yet?"

"Yes sir; she was to leave for Croydon in Mr Huskisson's car soon after we left Scudamore Hall."

Richardson looked at the clock. "The next plane leaves in a little over half an hour. If you break the speed limit you may just do it. It's worth trying."

Even while his chief was speaking Lawrence was stowing his papers safely away in an inside pocket and was halfway to the door. "I'll do it," he said.

"Good luck to you," called Richardson before the door was shut.

Lawrence did do it. By good luck his car evaded all traffic jams and even overtook the passenger car which conveyed travellers to the aerodrome. He was in time to catch Pauline before she climbed into the machine and to hand over to her the papers to be conveyed to M. Goron of the Sûreté Générate.

"You are not coming, monsieur?" she asked Lawrence.

"No, mademoiselle; but we can trust Monsieur Goron to pass on any information useful to us through our colleague, Mr Dallas."

"Yes, you can trust him to do that."

"And the documents could not be in safer hands than yours," said Lawrence with unwonted gallantry: he had been converted by this nimble-witted young Frenchwoman to confidence in her sex. "The note was discovered in a pocket of the monk's robe that we found in that trunk this morning and the newspaper is what the sandals were wrapped in."

"And I may examine them?"

"Certainly."

There was no time for more; the engines were turning over; the cry of "Stand back, please," came from the chief attendant at the aerodrome. It was a necessary warning, for at that moment the engines increased their speed and drove a fierce blast upon the onlookers; their roar prevented any further conversation; the draught they caused seemed strong enough to tear up the grass by the roots; the plane was now skidding along the field and imperceptibly its wheels ceased to revolve: it was in the air.

Left to herself, Pauline took the documents from their envelope and scrutinized them, paying particular attention to the copy of the *Daily Mail*. The journey from Croydon to Le Bourget was uneventful. Pauline took a vacant taxi and drove straight to Goron's office. To her great joy she found him at work.

"Behold me, monsieur. I come from the British shore laden with spoil. First let me ask you to telephone for your English colleague, Monsieur Dallas. I have here something that will be of particular interest to him."

"I am expecting him at any moment. We have been busy and he has gone to eat. What have you?"

"First I bring back with me the fur coat which is Monsieur Henri's property."

"Then they have discovered the murderer of Miss Gask?"

"Not yet, monsieur. Margaret Gask was not wearing this coat when she was killed."

"Then when was it found?"

"Well, it's a story of a broken romance. Shall I tell it to you now, or shall we wait for Monsieur Dallas?"

Scarcely had she spoken when the door opened to admit Dallas. After the usual greetings she opened the suitcase and displayed the fur coat. Dallas' English phlegm was proof against any show of emotion. He took it to the window and began to examine it.

"No, monsieur, you are wasting your time. You will find no bloodstains on it."

"Come, mademoiselle," said Goron; "you have whetted our appetite for your story and you are baulking it."

"My story is soon told. Poor Mr Huskisson, whom you suspected of being a double-dyed villain, is cleared. He, like Monsieur Henri and others, was seduced by Margaret's charms into thinking her a blameless angel. When he discovered that she was, to put it baldly, nothing but a common thief it was a great shock to him. He had persuaded her to let him restore this coat to Monsieur Henri, but before he had done so she was murdered. Partly out of fear and partly out of chivalry towards the woman he had loved, he had kept it hidden. You, monsieur," she said to Dallas, "will be pleased to know that it was through your Mr Spofforth that it was found."

Dallas listened with growing interest to her story of the cloakroom ticket, but Goron, on the other hand, was drumming on the table with his fingertips in his impatience to hear about the other things she had brought. Pauline watched him with a twinkle in her eye and then passed him the unsealed envelope which she had received from Lawrence. "I fancy that these papers may be of interest to you."

Goron drew out first the copy of the continental *Daily Mail* and after a quick glance at each page he strode over to his safe and took out of it an envelope containing a scrap of newspaper. This he fitted to the page from which a strip had been torn off.

"It is it," he exclaimed with excitement. "This is the paper from which the strip was torn and it was used by the murderer of the senator, Monsieur Salmond. Where did you get it?"

"I will tell you, but first I have one other piece of news about the coat. In a pocket we found this visiting card of Monsieur Salmond."

She passed it to Goron, who said, "My deduction was right. That woman and Monsieur Salmond were acquainted and we shall find that my other deduction is correct—that the two were killed by the same person. Now tell us where you found this newspaper and this bank note."

Pauline related the story of the tin trunk and was pleased to see that for once Dallas showed by his quick breathing that his interest had been thoroughly aroused.

"This butler," he explained to Goron, "is an ex-convict liberated from Dartmoor a few months ago."

"But surely a monk's robe would be a strange thing for an ex-convict in your country to have in his possession."

Dallas explained that between the butler and Douglas Oborn, the brother of James, there was a secret understanding. "Depend upon it," he concluded, "they connived at the escape of James from England; but they can help him no longer now, seeing that he is in your country."

"Now that we believe him to have been the murderer of Monsieur Salmond it is more important than ever that we should find him."

"Is it possible," asked Dallas, "that the father abbot at that monastery is shielding him from pursuit? We know that he is fertile in inventing excuses, sufficient to deceive an innocent ecclesiastic."

"It would be very easy for them to hide him," said Pauline, "if he had won their sympathies."

"Let us think," said Goron. "Presumably this same man was staying with Mademoiselle Saulnois at Cannes last November. He returns again now and takes refuge in the monastery. Did he get into touch with the father abbot in November? I think that the answer to that question is no. The abbot and every monk that I questioned declared emphatically that they had never seen him until he sought their hospitality a few days ago. If it had not been true they would have either evaded the question or declined point-blank to answer it. Therefore, if he was a complete stranger and they now know from us that he is an ordinary criminal, they are not likely to be hiding him."

"As a monk's habit appears to be his favourite disguise, would it not be well to widen the quest to cover all religious houses?" said Pauline.

"That is being done," said Goron, "but he had thrown away his monk's robes; it was found by a gendarme rolled up behind a hedge. However," he added, "I refuse to be discouraged. This paper that you have brought me supplies the missing clue that I need in my evidence against the murderer of Monsieur Salmond."

"And the bank note," suggested Pauline.

Goron examined the bank note for the first time. "I myself will go to the Credit Lyonnais; it may be possible to trace the fact that it was paid out to Monsieur Salmond. I don't think that it is usual for them to stamp their notes."

"I am wondering," said Dallas, "whether I am of any further use here. When James Oborn is caught you will detain him for a murder committed within your jurisdiction. If you want my corroboration I can always come over again."

"It is complicated, my friend," said Goron, "because although we believe them to belong to James Oborn, the newspaper and the note were found in your country in the possession of that ex-convict."

"Who is now dangerously ill," put in Pauline.

"I think you are right," said Goron. "You can really do more good now in your own country by watching over that man and getting his statement as soon as he recovers. I have here many hours of reading in this mass of stuff that came in while we have been away at Cannes."

"I will telephone to my chief in London and take his instructions."

Dallas demanded London and gave the number, Whitehall 1212, but had to wait some minutes before the call could be put through. When at last an English voice responded he asked for

Mr Richardson of the C.I.D. The response was immediate. Dallas explained as shortly as possible the position of the enquiry in Paris and asked for instructions whether he should continue to wait in Paris until James Oborn was found or return to London. The answer was prompt and clear. He was to remain in Paris and assist in the hunt for James Oborn.

Chapter Twenty-Six

DALLAS RETURNED to Goron's room. "My tidings may not be altogether to you taste, Monsieur Goron, but the instructions I have received by telephone are clear. I am to remain in Paris to assist you, if required, in tracing that rascal, James Oborn."

Goron slapped his thigh. "That is good news; after all, you have become one of us. Your colleagues in London can quite well take a statement from the injured butler as soon as he is well enough to be questioned. I am now reading a further account of the life of the Marquis de Crémont. Between us I feel sure that we shall make our coup."

Pauline Coulon had been silent. She now said, "Listen, messieurs; I recall a conversation that I once had with the dead woman. I had been giving her good advice and telling her how to resist the temptations put in her way by the buyers of American houses and she said, 'Well, when I've had my fling, if they pinch me I can always retire to a convent and make my peace with God.' 'In your own country?' I asked. 'Oh no,' she replied. 'I know of a certain convent in the Gers, the loveliest spot in France, where I can be quite happy milking the cows, plucking the chickens...' 'And killing the pigs?' I said. 'Well, no; I might draw the line at that: they squeal so dreadfully.' She went on talking in that strain and I put it down to her love of mischief, but she did say that the chaplain to this convent was a fellow countryman."

"*Tiens!*" exclaimed Goron. "There may be something worth following up in those remarks."

"Where is the Gers?" asked Dallas.

"Between Toulouse and Bayonne. It is truly a Godforsaken country."

"You mean a desert?"

"No; the land is good if it were cultivated, but the greater part of it has been deserted by the French peasants and left to Italians, who exhaust the land and then drift away to the towns. The French peasant farmers can get no labour and so the soil reverts day by day. The last time I passed through it I talked to one of these peasant farmers about the land and we drank an *apéritif* at my expense in the village inn. He took me by the arm and pointed to a church in the next village. 'There,' he said, 'you can see the whole church down to its foundations, but when I was a boy you could see nothing lower than the spire; the rains have washed away all the hills between and that is why the soil has become unprofitable.'"

"Are there monasteries there?" asked Dallas.

"Yes, and the monks contrive to make a fat living out of their farms. I know a Trappist brotherhood, mostly English or Irish, who converse only by signs."

Dallas pricked up his ears. "That sounds a likely hiding place for our man."

With his usual enthusiasm Goron jumped at this new clue. "To the Gers we will go ourselves and not leave it to my subordinates. Will you come with us, mademoiselle, in case we fall into difficulties with the grim ladies who rule the convents?"

"You must not call the superiors grim. If they rule their convents well no doubt they appear to be severe, but the work they do is of inestimable value," said Pauline, who was a good Catholic. "But after I have seen Monsieur Henri I will gladly come with you." Her face fell. "Ah! There may be one difficulty. My expenses?"

Goron laughed. "How like a woman," he said. "Had you been of our sex, mademoiselle, you would have said nothing about expenses until the day of reckoning. Then you would have bounced into the room, planked a vast account sheet under my nose and demanded instant settlement. As it is, I can see that you would like to have a settlement since human life is always uncertain, but you make no demands; you trust to your charming personality and stand there with open hand. When I have had time to glance through your account it shall be settled without delay."

"I have it here, monsieur."

"Good; then tomorrow before we start for the Gers settlement will be made. The expenses of our trip I will be responsible for; our car will leave in the morning at nine-thirty."

"Then all I have to do is to make my peace with Monsieur Henri. May I soften his heart by restoring to him his fur coat?"

"Certainly. The person who stole it is dead and cannot appear before any French tribunal. Before you go, mademoiselle, you must listen to what I have to tell. As I said, I have been reading a report from a member of my staff who has succeeded in tracing the earlier history of that *soi-distant* Marquis de Crémont. This is his career. His real name is Edouard Cottin; he was born in the department of the Aisne in the year 1900. From his early childhood he was noted as a liar and a thief and in order to cure him of these propensities he was sent to a priest who kept him by his side for three years, but he could do nothing with him. Then he entered the military school at Fontainebleau whence he graduated as sub-lieutenant. While in garrison he made friends with the monks of a neighbouring monastery and this became a subject of chaff with his comrades. He resolved to desert. He came into touch with a Dominican monk who persuaded him to take the cowl. He entered the monastery and played his cards so well that the prior appointed him quêteur, the brother selected to seek subscriptions for the monastery. Money was a temptation that he could not resist. He returned from his first mission several thousand francs short in his accounts. It was a favourable moment for disappearing. He went to the prior and informed him that he had come into a large fortune but dared not claim it, since technically he was a deserter from his regiment. Would the prior protect him? On this the prior gave him introductions and credentials from the monastery. His first act was to obtain 200,000 francs from the bankers by false pretences and he then threw off his monk's habit and became the Marquis de Tolosant and by scheming and false pretences was able to gain large sums of money and to pose as a man of fashion. He eluded our police by going to Italy, where he placed himself under the protection of a venerable French priest who vouched for him. He then began to fleece his new friends by wonderful schemes for getting rich quick. Then he decamped from Rome and returned to France as the Marquis de Crémont. Since that time he has been successful in a series of lucrative robberies, but as you know, we have him now lodged safely in prison."

"He is just the man," said Dallas, "who would suggest to his confederates the disguise of a monk's robe. Do you think it worth while visiting the monastery in which this blackguard first took the cowl?"

"That has already been done. In tracing his history backwards my people have interviewed everyone with whom he was ever connected. The prior of that monastery now knows his true history."

"It was a fine piece of work," said Dallas.

"It took some time, you understand. For months we have been trying to trace this man's criminal career."

"I think, however," said Dallas, "that I should like to have an interview with that prior."

"Oh, you British! You must begin at the beginning and go on to the bitter end in all your cases. Very well, we will see the prior tomorrow morning before going on to the Gers. Meanwhile I will see the people who sent in this report."

"And I will see Monsieur Henri," said Pauline, taking up the suitcase in which she had replaced the fur coat.

"And I will go to clear up the arrears of work piled on my table," said Dallas.

Punctually to the minute the car moved off next morning and took a southerly course.

"The monastery we are bound for lies somewhere between Fontainbleau and St Cyr," said Goron, "but I have full directions how to get there." He pulled a paper from his pocket and studied it.

In spite of his boast they had three times lost their way in the maze of roads that radiated in every direction before they finally arrived at the monastery. Built originally as a country house in the reign of Louis XV, it was externally a most unlikely building for a monastery. One expected every vista in the park to be graced by female figures in eighteenth-century costumes, whereas in fact such female figures as there were had dispensed with costumes altogether: marble does not look well in muslin.

Leaving Pauline in the car, the two men sought admittance at the main entrance. The delay seemed interminable, but this was because visitors were expected to knock at a postern gate further along the façade. At last a servitor in monk's habit answered their summons and after some coming and going permitted them to enter the building.

The prior was a man of between fifty and sixty, hale and hearty for his age and full of worldly wisdom in spite of the narrow circle in which he lived.

"We have come," said Goron, "on a rather unpleasant duty, namely, to enquire about a man who was for some time a member of your fraternity—a man named Edouard Cottin." The name produced a shiver from the prior, but he did not interrupt. "You will be able to correct any slips in our information, which says that Cottin was living here in the year 1922." The prior nodded without speaking. He was waiting to hear how far the information of his visitors went. "I feel sure that we can count upon you to help the ends of justice and to answer such questions as we may put to you that do not affect the religious side of your house." Still the prior waited. "Our first question is, did this young man leave your fraternity under a cloud?"

"Not exactly."

"He had appropriated funds given to the Church, I believe."

"Alas, monsieur, that is so. He was our quéteur and it was not until he had left us that we discovered that his accounts had been falsified."

"Then you did not expel him?"

"No; he came to me and said that he had been left a fortune by his uncle on certain conditions but that he dared not claim it because he would have to confess that he was a deserter from the army. On this I gave him certain introductions and he left us."

"You know that since then he has plunged lower and lower into crime?"

"Yes, monsieur; some time after he left us I began to receive complaints from the people to whom I had given him the letters of introduction. Some of them talked of prosecution, but he escaped them by leaving the country."

"Have you seen or heard of him since?" asked Goron.

The prior hesitated. "It is painful to have to answer such questions, monsieur. We are not made judges of human delinquencies."

"Quite so, but surely you feel bound to help in keeping your country free from crimes and it is a crime to prey upon honest members of the community."

After struggling with himself for a moment the prior said, "You must understand, monsieur, that with us it is the soul, even of the most degraded, that counts before all else. The man Edouard Cottin is one who with many good points in his favour is so constituted that he cannot withstand the temptation of money. But I will tell you all I know. About two years ago he came to me, arriving late at night, and begged me to take him in as a penitent. He confessed and I, considering that his penitence was genuine, consented to admit him. He remained with us for some weeks and left of his own accord."

"Did he leave suddenly?"

The prior reluctantly admitted that he did.

"Did he leave any luggage behind him?"

"Yes."

"May we examine it?"

"It is no longer with us. Shortly after he left a priest who was a foreigner but came armed with credentials called for his luggage. We discussed Edouard and from what he told me I judged that this time he was really penitent. He was with this reverend father in his monastery."

"You gave up the luggage?"

"I did."

"And you know the whereabouts of the monastery?"

"I found afterwards that it was non-existent."

"What did the luggage consist of?"

"A trunk."

"Was it heavy?"

"Fairly so."

"How did the priest take it away?"

"In his car."

"This gentleman," said Goron, indicating Dallas, "is a British police officer in search of a criminal who is believed to have been associated with Cottin in various doubtful transactions and it is very probable that the priest who called for Cottin's luggage is the man in whom he is interested. You are quite sure you can give us no further information? Where was this monastery supposed to be?"

"In the Puy de Dôme, but I have satisfied myself that there is no such monastery in that department."

"But the credentials that he brought with him. Did you verify these?"

"The credentials purported to be signed by the father abbot of the Monastery of St Gilles in the Gers. I have written to him, but he denies all knowledge of the person in question. I have kept his letter; I will show it to you." He was gone for two or three minutes and then returned, carrying a letter in his hand, which he handed to Goron, who read it and passed it to Dallas, saying, "The father abbot's name is Collet—to us a significant coincidence."

Chapter Twenty-Seven

HAVING PUMPED the prior dry by their questions, they thanked him warmly and rejoined Pauline Coulon, who had been waiting in the car outside. They imparted to her the few facts elicited by their questions to the prior.

"It is still mysterious, but something tells me that we are approaching the end," was her comment. "I suppose that our next port of call will be the monastery at St Gilles."

"It will," said Goron.

Each was busy with his own thoughts and there was no conversation during the journey. As they drew nearer to the Gers,

Dallas looked about him with renewed interest. Even his untutored eye could mark the signs of depopulation and of deterioration of the land buildings. It was a poverty-stricken country but an excellent resort for anyone who wished to disappear from the world.

After enquiring their way from the few people they met on the road Goron remarked, "It is not surprising that people shrug their shoulders when asked about the Gers. It is quite the last place I could bear to be banished to. I should think that the statistics of insanity were high in this department. The public buildings, no doubt, are chiefly lunatic asylums."

"Or homes for idiots," amended Pauline. "Do you think that the Monastery of St Gilles really exists?"

"According to the last directions we got," said Goron, "we should now be nearing the place. What about that big building away there a little to the left? We'll try it."

As they drew near it and noted the fortress-like architecture and the plaster walls defaced with patches from which the covering had peeled off, even Goron began to lose heart. Not a soul was to be seen; the walks were overgrown with grass; there was not a sound from any living thing. The outbuildings, stables and all were in ruins.

"The place is deserted; it is falling into ruin."

"All the more likely to be what we are in search of," said Dallas.

They had come to the front of the ruined stable and there, staring at them, was a car of the most modern type standing under the ruinous roof of the coach house, which could not be shut because its great doors had rotted on their hinges. It looked like a costly jewel round the neck of a beggar woman.

"Ah!" exclaimed Goron. "This is beginning to look like business. Monks don't run about in expensive modern cars."

"Neither do they let their house fall into rack and ruin," said Pauline.

"Shall we leave the car here and go to the door on foot?" said Dallas.

"I think that will be our best plan," agreed Goron.

While they were getting out Pauline lowered her voice. "Have you ever seen a religious house with no cross or other indication on it to show what it is?"

"*Tiens!*" said Goron. "What an eye a woman has for little details of that kind. Come, Mr Dallas, you and I will probe this mystery. You will be quite safe here, mademoiselle; you have always the motor horn with which to sound an alarm."

The two men made their way towards the front entrance of the rambling château. A rusty bellpull of ancient pattern invited them to ring. The iron creaked as they set the bell in motion; the clapper produced a cracked sound which was loud enough to reach every corner of the property. After a pause of nearly a minute a little spy hole was opened in the heavy oaken door and an eye was brought to the aperture. It was baffling to note that the spy hole was closed again and that nothing further seemed likely to happen. Goron pulled the bell chain fiercely; he had set his teeth now and intended to go on ringing until the tocsin produced somebody; but the second summons was enough: the door was opened a few inches and a burly hirsute monk confronted them.

"Excuse me for disturbing you," said Goron. "We have come to see Father Collet."

"The reverend father is away."

"I'm sorry for that, because it will entail our waiting here until his return; but in a big property like this you can no doubt give us hospitality."

"Pardon, monsieur, but our fraternity is debarred by rule from giving hospitality to visitors."

Being a man of action, Goron unobtrusively slipped his foot against the door to prevent it from being shut upon them.

"You will excuse us for coming in," he said. "We have some questions to ask about Father Collet."

The man's shifty eyes glanced from one to the other: he was measuring the chances of being able to shut the door in their faces. "It is against the rule of our fraternity to admit laymen."

Goron felt that the moment had come for displaying the iron hand that had been concealed in velvet. "Stand back," he commanded Shifty Eyes. "I belong to a fraternity, too—the fraternity responsible for law and order in this country and I mean to search this building from roof to basement."

"I must call my senior," said the monk. Finding it impossible to shut the door in their faces, he shuffled off down the passage.

"Have you a pistol?" whispered Goron to Dallas.

"No; I never carry one."

"*Mon Dieu!* You English! Follow me."

He started in pursuit of the monk with Dallas at his heels—Dallas, who had not attended the evening boxing class at Scotland Yard for nothing. They caught up with Shifty Eyes as he was opening a door on the left of the gallery. It gave upon what was obviously the kitchen of the old château and there they found a group of some half-dozen men in monks' habit.

"Hands up!" rapped out Goron, whipping out a pistol and covering the group. Thus taken by surprise, the men obeyed. They had been engaged in the innocent pursuit of cooking a meal; the table was covered with dishes and food. A little rat-faced man rushed forward as bold as brass.

"What is the meaning of this?" he demanded in French.

"It means that I represent the law and I intend to search this building from garret to cellar."

"What are you looking for?"

"We are looking for a fugitive from justice—an Englishman."

"You won't find him here," sneered Rat Face.

Dallas had been staring hard at one of the monks. He now signed to him to come forward. "You are James Oborn," he said in English. "I recognise you from the photograph on your card of identity."

"I am James Oborn, but I am not a fugitive from justice."

"At any rate there are matters in your life these last weeks which you will find it difficult to explain away." He turned to Goron and said in French, "This is our man."

Goron made a rapid survey of the monks; they were a ruffianly-looking crowd and they numbered seven to two. He whispered to Dallas, "Quick! Hurry to Mademoiselle and ask her to find the nearest constabulary station and get them to send up a reinforcement for us: fortunately she can drive a car."

When Dallas returned from his errand he found the ecclesiastics seated in a row along one side of the refectory table. His eyes had never beheld a more forbidding collection.

"Let us lock these men in and take our friend into another room to answer questions," said Goron.

It was not to be accomplished without protest. At first Oborn refused doggedly to move. "You can ask as many questions as you like in the presence of my friends here. They don't understand English."

"No nonsense," said Goron; "you know this house. Lead the way to a room where we can talk without eavesdroppers and be quick about it." He was holding the persuasive pistol in his hand with the finger upon the trigger.

Thus persuaded, Oborn led the way in silence and passed through a door on the right of the passage, closely followed by Goron and Dallas. The room was small and smelt of damp. The furniture was deeply covered in dust.

"Do you claim to be the father abbot of this establishment?" was Goron's first question.

"I do not."

"Then where is the abbot?"

"I don't know. He is absent, but we are never told where he goes. If it is the abbot you are looking for, what can you want with me?"

"We want to know something of your own movements since the beginning of last November."

"They are soon told, monsieur. I was in England."

"Were you not in Paris on November seventh?" put in Goron.

"I was not. I was staying with a relation in Hoxton. I can give you the address if you are curious and there are plenty of witnesses who can prove that I was there." Goron showed his disappointment, but Dallas changed his mode of attack.

"On December nineteenth you were in Kingston-on-Thames, driving a car with a false number. You knocked down a woman and did not stop."

Oborn shrugged his shoulders. "If that was true it would not be a case for extradition."

"Where did you spend the night of December nineteenth?"

"In Yorkshire. I was on my way there when I had the accident you mention. I was in a hurry, as I had to meet someone on the way."

"That someone was your brother Douglas?"

"It was."

"You know a man named Alfred Curtis who is in service as a butler. Why was he taking care of an iron trunk containing clothing belonging to you?"

"Alfred Curtis is not holding any property of mine."

"Why did your car bear the same number as your brother's?"

"Just a freak on our part."

"As you say, that is not an extraditable offence; but your statements as to your movements in November and December will have to be verified. You have no objection to returning to England with me for this to be done?"

"It would be very inconvenient."

Goron now took up the interrogation. "If you had nothing to hide or to fear why did you escape from St Augustin House at Fréjus?"

"Well, it's a free country and I was in no way bound to stay there. I was anxious to get back here."

"Why did you go to Nice?"

"I had business there."

"But you pretended to be a Spanish refugee. Were you staying as a guest with Mademoiselle Saulnois in November?"

"I was not."

"Well," said Goron, "I must ask you to come to Paris with me and see if Mademoiselle Saulnois recognises you."

"I can assure you I have never met the lady you speak of, but I will come and you will see for yourself that she will not know me."

"In any case you will accompany us as soon as we have completed the searching of this house."

"I shall yield to force majeure, of course, but I shall lodge a protest against this high-handed proceeding."

"As many protests as you like. We are only doing our official duty. Perhaps you will do the honours of the house by showing us over it."

The toot of a motor horn was heard at this juncture. Dallas went quickly to the window and cried, "Here are your friends the constabulary, monsieur; certainly Mademoiselle Coulon has wasted no time."

"That's good," said Goron. "Now, monsieur, we need not trouble you to come over the house with us. You can join your friends in the kitchen."

It fell to Dallas to open the front door and admit two big men in constabulary uniform. To them Goron briefly explained the situation. The newcomers showed startled surprise. They had regarded the monastery as being a building to which no suspicion could attach.

Oborn was conducted to the kitchen and the door was unlocked to admit him. Meanwhile a quiet injunction was given to one of the constables to keep an eye upon the occupants and allow no one to pass out. The other constable was asked to accompany the search party round the house.

As they went along the gallery Goron said, "I suppose that you had no idea that this house was anything but what it pretended to be."

"No, monsieur; we understood that the monks were very poor, but they used to give freely to the local charities when they could afford it."

"How long have they been here?" asked Dallas.

The constable reflected. "It must have been nearly three years ago when they came."

"You saw that man that we were questioning as you came in; is he the father abbot?"

"No, the father abbot is a taller man."

Most of the rooms they visited were poorly furnished bedrooms; beyond the fact that they sorely needed a duster there was nothing remarkable about them. The constable was assuming the air of "I told you so" when Goron pulled open a door which admitted them to a suite of rooms furnished almost lavishly—a bedroom and a study.

"These must be the rooms of the father abbot," commented Dallas. "They look as if they haven't been used for some weeks."

Under the windows of the study were two old oak chests. Goron lifted the lid of one of them and called to Dallas. "They could scarcely have feared either constabulary or thieves."

He displayed a confused medley of silver plate. He examined the hallmark. "This, unless I am much mistaken, is all stolen property."

Dallas gave but a half-hearted glance at his companion's discovery, for he was busy looking at some photographs that he had discovered on the mantelpiece. "This solves most of the mystery," he exclaimed. "This is the father abbot and I know this man as Douglas Oborn."

Chapter Twenty-Eight

SUPERINTENDENT LAWRENCE entered his chief's room with the expression he wore whenever he was the bearer of tidings. It was an expression that would not be denied and there was besides an element of self-elation in it. Richardson knew it well and prepared himself a little ruefully to listen. He would very gladly have been left alone with his papers for the rest of the morning.

"I'm sorry to interrupt you, sir, but I think I ought to show you this. It has just come from Mademoiselle Coulon in Paris."

Richardson's brow cleared. "What does she say?" he asked.

Lawrence began to read the report aloud. Richardson's fingers drummed on the table. "Don't bother to read the whole thing through. Just give me the gist of it," he said.

"Very good, sir. She says that the newspapers that she took over—the paper in which the sandals were wrapped—will prove to be an important link in the chain of evidence against the murderer of Monsieur Salmond."

"You mean that the scrap of paper which Monsieur Goron holds was torn from it?"

"Yes sir."

"And it was found in a trunk belonging to Alfred Curtis. When will he be well enough to be questioned?"

"I thought, sir, that with your approval I would go to Scudamore Hall this morning and see what the latest medical report is."

"Yes, and you might put a little gentle pressure on the doctor. These country practitioners have one weakness in common. They like to enhance their importance by raising medical objections to their patients being questioned: they don't like to be left out of the fun."

"Very good, sir; I'll start at once."

The run from New Scotland Yard to Scudamore Hall could be covered in under an hour. As Lawrence went up the drive he descried the doctor's car drawn up at the steps leading to the front door. He determined to hang about until its owner made his appearance. He had not long to wait. The doctor had a professional trick of bolting into his car like a frightened rabbit and making off as if every hellhound in the neighbourhood was baying at his heels, but no escape was possible when he had to deal with the myrmidons of the law and he knew it.

The plain question put to him—could Alfred Curtis be questioned that morning?—left him no choice but to answer yes or no. Obviously if the answer was no, a reason must be given and the doctor desired above all things to be on terms with the police authorities.

"I don't think that I, as his doctor, need withhold permission. He recovered consciousness yesterday. He has, fortunately, a skull as thick as a chimpanzee's; the crack he had would have killed most men. If you see that he begins to wander in his replies it would be better to break off, but so far he can give you lucid answers. Would you like me to be present?"

"Yes," said Lawrence. "I think it would be as well. You can make a little sign to me if you think that I'm doing him any harm and, incidentally, you might give a hint to his employer, Mr Forge, that the fewer people present the better."

"I quite understand that," said the doctor.

At that moment the front door opened and Forge himself appeared on the steps. "I saw your car from the window," he said to Lawrence, "and I came down to ask you whether I can be of any use."

"The doctor has given me permission to interview Curtis; he thinks that if he himself is present there will be no danger to the patient if he is questioned."

"I see. Of course you wouldn't want me to be present?"

"No," said the doctor decisively. "The fewer people present the better."

"Well," said Forge, "then all I can do is to wait to hear the result of your interview."

"That is all, I think," said Lawrence.

The doctor led the way to the bedroom and signed to the nurse that she could leave them. They found Curtis propped up with pillows with a bandage round his head, but so far as could be seen he appeared to be little the worse for his accident.

"Well, Curtis," said Lawrence, "you know me?"

"Yes, Mr Lawrence. So you've tumbled to it that this fall of mine from the upper floor wasn't an accident?" Lawrence was taken back for a moment, but he made no sign. "What was it then?" he asked.

"It was a dirty trick someone played on me by unhooking the ladder while I was in the loft."

"I'll have to examine that ladder and see whether that could be done," said Lawrence.

"It could be done quite easily. You see, the ladder hooks on to an iron bar: anyone could make it unsafe by shifting the ladder two or three inches and you wouldn't notice that from the top."

"You don't mean that someone did this on purpose?" said Lawrence.

"I do, and I bet I know who it was—that fellow Spofforth. He's always dogging my footsteps and he knew I was up there."

"But Spofforth wouldn't do anything like that: he'd know how dangerous it was to anyone who happened to be in the loft."

"Well, it's up to you people to find out who did it."

"Certainly, that shall be done," said Lawrence; "and now I want you to answer one or two questions. I must administer the usual caution that your answers will be taken down in writing..."

"And may be used in evidence against me. I know all the usual formulas; you needn't waste time over them."

"You went up to that loft because you had hidden an iron trunk up there containing a certain disguise?"

"That trunk was locked," said Curtis. "Who's been tampering with it?"

"Never mind that. What I want to know is, what were you doing with the clothing of a monk?"

Curtis fell back as usual on impudence. "I suppose you've never heard of private theatricals; these ecclesiastical habits are often used in them: they are so easy to put on and take off and they form a wonderful disguise."

Lawrence looked at the doctor for a sign of disapproval, but found his expression quite reassuring, so he determined to run some risk.

"This disguise," he said deliberately, "was worn by a murderer."

Curtis showed signs of agitation. "You're talking through your hat," he said.

"I assure you I'm doing nothing of the kind. That trunk contained evidence sufficient to hang a man and it is your trunk."

"The trunk isn't mine. I'm looking after it for someone."

"Name?"

There was no answer; the patient had leaned back on his pillows: the doctor stepped forward to look at him, nodded to Lawrence and said, "He's all right."

Then the butler was given the gift of tongues and what he said was quite unfit for polite ears; he was apostrophising some unnamed person and telling him what he thought of his disposition and habits. The doctor looked shocked, but Lawrence seemed inclined to purr with satisfaction.

"Will you give me the name now?" he asked.

Curtis leaned forward from his pillows and spoke earnestly. "Will you swear, sir, that what you tell me is true; that that trunk contained evidence proving that the man it belonged to is a murderer?"

"I can swear it," said Lawrence.

"Then I'll tell you. The person that trunk belongs to is staying in this house and his name is Douglas Oborn. I can see now who shifted that ladder and nearly cracked my skull—he meant to crack it and do me in—it was that swine."

Lawrence broke in with his purring voice. "Perhaps it would be better if I took down a statement from you. You can read it over before you sign it and see that it is in accord with what you know."

Lawrence was gifted with the pen of a ready writer; he jotted down the statement in the man's own words; he read it over to him and passed his fountain pen to him for his signature. The doctor leaned forward in order not to miss a word of what was said.

"Yes sir; that's all right: those are my very words. That's the first time in my life that I've ever given a pal away, but there it is—when a bloke tries to do one in I've done with him. Besides, an honest burglar is one thing and a murderer's another." He signed the statement in a shaky hand; Lawrence folded it and stowed it in an inside breast pocket.

"Now, Curtis, all you have to do is to lie there and get well. You can leave all the rest to me. Good-bye for the present."

As they went down the stairs the doctor looked at his watch and said, "Gosh! This has made me late for my other patients, but I wouldn't have missed it: it's an experience to remember."

The noise of an altercation somewhere on the ground floor caught their attention. Two or three men were talking at once in the library. The doctor paused on his way to the front door, listening, and said, "There's some sort of a row going on in that room. I suppose I shall have to miss this part of the entertainment, but you'll want to go in and quell the disturbance. I'll let myself out. I shall have to break every speed limit on the way."

Lawrence waved good-bye to him and turned to the library door and threw it open. Four men seemed to be talking at once—Forge, Spofforth, Huskisson and Oborn—each trying to drown the other.

"You're the very man we want, Mr Lawrence," said Forge as he caught sight of him. "These guests of mine are making the wildest accusations against each other and you are the only man who can deal with them."

Before Lawrence could say a word Huskisson stepped forward. Pointing to Oborn, he said, "I charge this man with having stolen my pocketbook and I insist on him being searched."

"It's damned impertinence," said Oborn. "Does he take me for a thief? I've never seen his pocketbook."

Lawrence looked from one to the other and caught a meaning look in Huskisson's face. "Have you any grounds for your suspicion, sir?"

"Yes, I have, and you can get the proof of my charge by searching him."

"I refuse to be searched," said Oborn, sticking out his lower jaw.

"Well, sir, then if this gentleman prefers a charge against you I must take you to the police station and let the inspector deal with it. We can start at once."

"It's a perfectly absurd charge and I shall not come," said Oborn.

"Well, sir, if the charge is a false one and you submit to being searched and nothing is found you can turn the tables on this gentleman and give him in charge for making a false accusation. The search would not be more than a formality."

Lawrence's quick eye caught sight of Oborn's hand creeping towards his hip pocket. Quick as lightning, he seized both the man's wrists.

"Catch hold," he said to Spofforth and with dexterous skill he slipped his hand into Oborn's hip pocket; he drew out a revolver. "A pistol?" he said. "Have you a firearms licence to carry this? No, I can see you haven't. You'll have to come with me to the police station, where we can go into the matter further."

Oborn looked wildly round as if measuring his chances of escape and then shrugged his shoulders. "All right," he said; "I'll go with you."

"There's more than one matter that you'll have to explain, such as how you came into possession of a monk's robe and sandals, and there may be other charges to prefer against you."

Huskisson stepped forward. "I think that you may find that pistol interesting, Inspector, if you compare the cartridges with those found in recent murder cases."

Oborn's pleasant manner fell from him like a cloak. He turned upon Huskisson and snarled, "You interfering devil! You and your pocketbook. Just wait until this business has been cleared up and then you'll see what's coming to you."

"A threat of murder, I think," said Huskisson to Lawrence. "Please make a note of it. Murder is becoming one of his hobbies."

Chapter Twenty-Nine

RICHARDSON had been awaiting the return of Superintendent Lawrence with impatience: so much depended upon a statement from Alfred Curtis. When the door opened to admit Lawrence he saw by his manner and his walk that he was bringing something of importance. He pushed back the papers that he had been reading and put out his hand for the paper which the superintendent was carrying.

"I thought you'd better read this, sir, before going any further," said Lawrence; "it contains a statement from Alfred Curtis. I didn't wait to have it typed, but I think you always find my handwriting legible."

"Yes, Mr Lawrence; I wish that all your subordinates in the department wrote as clearly as you do."

The statement read,

"I, Alfred Curtis, have known Douglas and James Oborn for nearly fifteen years. I first met them when I was employed as a manservant in their father's house. Then I lost sight of them until about three years ago, when to my surprise I met James Oborn in the shop of Hyam Fredman. We were both on the same errand—disposing of goods to the best advantage. Fredman was a difficult customer to handle in the matter of values. James Oborn did his business first and when I came out I found him waiting for me outside. He said he could offer me a job and he took me away to lunch with him. The job was to act as a messenger in disposing of stuff to Fredman and he assured me it would be safer than trying to crack cribs myself. I was to be paid a percentage. During the past three years I have disposed of a good deal of stuff in this way and that is how I met Margaret Gask. She was sent to find me with a letter from Oborn and I had to introduce her to Fredman. Most of the stuff came in small parcels, one at a time, from France and was brought to me by James Oborn himself, Margaret Gask or a man called Arthur Graves. I often wondered why no one was ever pinched, but on one occasion Margaret Gask let out that the chief of the whole lot was head of a monastery, which, she said, was the safest disguise that could be thought of and he could always hide any of them. Then, last November, James Oborn told me to apply for this job at the Hall and gave me a forged reference. I understood that we were to do some jobs round the neighbourhood. In December Margaret Gask arrived as a guest and some days later Douglas Oborn followed. His coming was a great surprise to me. I opened the front door in answer to a ring and he stood on the doorstep. At first I didn't recognize him, but he said, 'You're Alfred Curtis; you remember me—Douglas Oborn.' I said, 'Good Lord! What are you doing here?' and he said, 'Come out to my car; I want you a minute.' Then he explained to me that he'd been invited as a guest by the old man, Mr Forge, but he'd got one bit of luggage that he wanted me to take out of his car and hide away somewhere. That is why he took his car into the shed and not into the garage. I couldn't stop, as I had to be on the spot to answer the front doorbell, but I carried the tin trunk into my pantry. Then I showed him in at the front door in the ordinary way."

The rest of the statement was in the form of question and answer.

(Q) "Do you know whether Margaret Gask and Douglas Oborn had met before their meeting at Scudamore Hall?"

(A) "Margaret Gask did not know him as Douglas Oborn but only as Father Collet."

(Q) "She knew that Collet was the head of this gang of international thieves?"

(A) "Oh yes, she knew that."

(Q) "Why did you put that tin trunk up in the loft?"

(A) "It was in the way in my pantry and Oborn wanted it hidden."

(Q) "Why were you getting it out on the day you met with your accident?"

(A) "Because Oborn was going to try to do a bunk in the monk's kit. You see, he's got a passport as Father Collet, besides one as Douglas Oborn."

(Q) "Do you know why he had come to England just now?"

(A) "Because France was getting too hot to hold him. His French pal had been pinched and he was afraid that he might split on him."

(Q) "Why should Douglas Oborn try to break your head?"

(A) "He brought me down an overcoat with bloodstains on it and told me to put it in the furnace. He said he was wearing it in a motor accident and that was how it got stained. Directly you told me that he was wanted for murder I guessed that he wanted that coat burned for another reason and as I was the only one that knew about it he thought that he'd better get rid of me. You see, we'd all been getting the wind up lately."

(Q) "Do you know who the overcoat belonged to?"

(A) "Yes, it belonged to Oborn himself."

(Q) "And did you burn it?"

(A) "No, I haven't had a chance yet. It's in the cupboard under the sink in my pantry."

Richardson finished reading and looked up at Lawrence. "Well, we're going ahead, Mr Lawrence."

"Yes sir, we are, and I have some further information for you." He described the scene in the library and Huskisson's ruse for getting Oborn searched. "Mr Huskisson told me afterwards, sir, that he had seen from the drive Oborn in his bedroom fingering something that he guessed was a pistol. The light was on and the blinds were not drawn. The following morning he contrived to bump into Oborn: he could plainly feel that he had a pistol in his hip pocket."

"It was a clever ruse of his to charge him with stealing his pocketbook and get him searched."

"It was, sir; I saw by his manner that he had a hidden reason and I played up to him: he wanted that pistol to be found."

"I suppose you brought Oborn along with you?"

"Yes sir, on a charge of having firearms without a licence. We have the bullet with which Fredman was killed and it fits the pistol."

"That's good enough: you can charge him with murder. Probably he killed both Margaret Gask and Fredman, but one will be enough to hold him on."

"If he is also the murderer of the French senator the question will arise on which side of the Channel he is to be tried."

"You had better send Dallas a wire saying that we have proof against Douglas Oborn of murder but not against James," said Richardson.

"I'll send that off at once, sir."

He left the room, but in less than a minute he was back again. "Here is a telegram, sir; it has just come from Dallas."

Richardson read, "James Oborn found stop not guilty of murder stop am crossing tonight with evidence. Dallas."

"We seem to be getting to the bottom of things, Mr Lawrence. You can charge Douglas Oborn with wilful murder and hold him until he appears before the magistrate. We shall have to wait to hear Dallas' story tomorrow morning."

"I forgot to mention, sir, that I told Spofforth to look for that coat and bring it along to us."

"Well, send him up to me when he does come."

Ten minutes later Spofforth was announced. He was carrying a brown paper parcel.

"What have you got there?" asked Richardson. "The coat?"

"Yes sir."

"Well, let's have a look at it."

The string was cut, the coat spread out on the table under the window. After a short examination under a lens Richardson pronounced, "This coat was worn by a person who was bleeding from the head and from the right side of the head. You can see the stains quite plainly, though some attempt has been made to wipe them away."

"Do you think, sir, that Miss Gask was wearing this coat when she was killed?"

"I think it likely," said Richardson cautiously. "She may have picked up the first coat she saw hanging in the hall and wrapped it round her; her murderer must have removed it because he thought it would incriminate him."

"Well, sir, if you'll excuse me I have to go back to Scudamore Hall to search Douglas Oborn's room and bring away anything that may be useful as evidence. What beats me is why he stayed on at the Hall all this time."

Richardson smiled. "That's where brains and cool courage came in. If he had run away we should have suspected him."

On the following morning four men were in conference in the chief constable's room at New Scotland Yard—M. Goron, Dallas, Lawrence and Richardson himself. Dallas had been relating the story of the raid upon the monastery in the Gers.

"As soon as I found the photographs of Douglas Oborn I realised that he must be the person we wanted. I saw then why neither Graves nor Margaret Gask knew a person of that name: he had posed to them as Father Collet."

"But the brother, James Oborn, also posed as a priest," said Richardson.

"On occasion, yes. The brothers apparently contrived alibis for one another, such as using the same registration number for both their cars. When confronted with James Oborn, Mademoiselle Saulnois said that he was not the man who had stayed with her at her villa on the Riviera."

"You are forgetting all the evidence we collected from the monastery," put in Goron. "There was much stolen property and a considerable sum of money in French notes. One of the lesser rascals offered to tell us all he knew in the hope of mitigating any sentence passed on him. From him we learned that they formed a gang of professional thieves—the monastery, of course, was a safe hiding place for them and their plunder. Douglas Oborn seems to have successfully maintained his authority as head of the gang."

"What I can't understand," confessed Richardson, "Is why he didn't return there to hide after the murder of the senator."

"He did," said Goron. "He lay low for a time and then came over to England under his true name."

"You are convinced, Monsieur Goron, that he murdered the senator, Monsieur Salmond?"

"Yes, I have managed to force an admission from De Crémont. I told him that Douglas Oborn was likely to be hanged in England for murder and I hinted that he had made a confession which was very damaging to De Crémont. Then the rascal gave tongue. It appears that Margaret Gask had made the acquaintance of Monsieur Salmond and that he had confided to her the fact that he didn't trust French banks but kept his money at home. Oborn suggested that he and De Crémont should crack the crib together, but finally they decided that Oborn as a holy father should call on the pretence of soliciting alms."

"Margaret Gask must have guessed that Father Collet, as she knew him, was the murderer," said Dallas.

"Yes, and it was to silence her forever that she was killed," said Richardson. "What we shall never know now is whether Douglas Oborn came over purposely to hunt her down or whether their meeting at Scudamore Hall was an accident. Obviously Fredman was killed because he knew who was the murderer of Margaret Gask."

"Douglas Oborn stands out as the most cold-blooded and calculating murderer that I've ever hunted down," said Dallas.

"What we have to decide," said Richardson, "is on which side of the Channel he is to be tried."

"If you are sure of a conviction in England I should vote for trying him here to save the expense and trouble of extradition," said Goron.

Thus it was that Douglas Oborn was tried and hanged in England for the murder of Hyam Fredman.

THE END

Made in the USA
Monee, IL
28 October 2021